Good-bye, Diablo

Gabi Adam

Good-bye, Diablo

Copyright © 2010 Gabi Adam
Original title: Diabolo Abscied
Cover photo © Bob Langrish
Cover layout: Stabenfeldt A/S

Typeset by Roberta L. Melzl
Editor: Bobbie Chase
Printed in Germany, 2010

ISBN: 978-1-934983-42-3

Stabenfeldt, Inc.
225 Park Avenue South
New York, NY 10003
www.pony4kids.com

Available exclusively through PONY.

I dedicate this book to all who have remained faithful to this
series throughout the years. Diablo and I say a heartfelt thank you,
and wish you many enjoyable hours of PONY book club reading!

— Gabi Adam, March 2009

Chapter 1

"Hey, I am so happy!" shouted fourteen-year-old Ricki Sulai, bubbling with excitement as she ran into her family's stable one beautiful, summer afternoon. Her friends Kevin Thomas, Cathy Sutherland, and Kevin's cousin Oliver Merrill, who had recently moved to the area, were already waiting for her.

"Happy? You looked completely crazy, the way you came flying in here just now." said Cathy. "What's gotten into you?"

"Oh!" Ricki grinned from ear to ear. "If you knew who just called me, and if you knew what I know, then you'd be as happy as I am," trilled Ricki.

"Come on, don't make it sound so mysterious. Tell us what's going on," Kevin, her boyfriend, urged, full of curiosity.

"I'm not saying anything. You'll find out soon enough." Ricki kissed Kevin on the cheek and then she gazed from one horse to the other. "Don't tell me you've already groomed them?"

"Of course. We were just waiting for you." Oliver looked at his watch. "Actually, you were supposed to be here half an hour ago."

"That's right, and considering you have to take all of two steps from your front door to here, you sure took your time," added Cathy.

"Women! You spend hours gossiping on the phone and forget that you have an appointment" teased Kevin. "In this case, to go riding with us."

"Kevin, get over it. I'm here now, and I already brushed Diablo till his coat shines. I just have to give him one more going over and then we can get going." Ricki ran into the tack room and returned with a soft brush.

"Now, my sweetie, move over and make room for me," she chided Diablo as she opened the door to his stall and nudged the beautiful black gelding to the side. "And don't you dare step on my foot again. My toes are still black and blue from the last time," she warned him, playfully pulling on his long mane as she quickly brushed the dust from his coat.

Her friends stood in the corridor watching her intently.

"What are you staring at? Don't you want to saddle up? If you wait much longer, I'll be done before you are." Ricki grinned, blowing a strand of hair off her forehead.

"Didn't you want to tell us something?"

"No."

"I don't get it," Cathy complained. "First you come in all excited, then you tease us about a mysterious phone call, and then say nothing. It's so unfair!"

Ricki laughed. "No it's not. I do have an amazing surprise for you, though, and if I tell you now, then I won't get to see your beaming faces later!"

"That's just great. Now I know everything," Cathy replied sarcastically, rolling her eyes. She gave up and went to get the saddle and tack for her dun horse, Rashid, who was thundering against the stall door with his front hoof.

"Okay, okay, I'm coming. Chill out, we're almost ready." She entered the stall shaking her head. "The way he's acting, you'd think he hadn't been ridden in months."

"I know what you mean. Sharazan has been acting strange today, too," commented Kevin, glancing at his roan.

Although Kevin and his mom had moved into the ranch house at Carlotta Mancini's Mercy Ranch, Kevin had continued to board his horse at the Sulais', which gave him an excuse to see Ricki on a daily basis. Besides, all the stalls at Mercy Ranch were meant to accommodate rescue horses.

"Then it's about time for us to get going." Oliver nodded at his cousin, and then he, too, started to saddle his mare, Miz Lizzy. She was sparkling white today, although she frequently had yellow spots on her coat. Her foal, Jessie, was easier to keep clean. She had a dark coat, and it would be a long time before she developed her mother's coloring.

"I think it's so cool that we can finally take Jessie with us on a ride." Ricki looked over the door of the stall at the pretty little foal. "I never thought she'd learn to follow on the lead so quickly."

Oliver smiled proudly. "Yeah, we did a good job training her, didn't we?"

"Absolutely!"

"Okay, I'm ready. Anybody else?" Cathy already was leading Rashid out of his stall and into the corridor.

"I'm almost done. If Sharazan would just keep his belly in, then maybe I could tighten the girth," groaned Kevin.

7

"Ha! You're lucky we don't have to put a girth around you!" joked Oliver, referring to his cousin's weakness for sweets.

"Very funny. I haven't gained any weight recently, have I? Hey, Ricki, am I fat?"

As an answer, his girlfriend just looked up at the ceiling innocently.

"Thanks a lot. Wow, you guys really know how to hurt a guy."

"Can we get going now?" urged Cathy. She'd been looking forward to the ride all day.

"Hey, you don't lose any weight riding, do you?" asked Kevin, worried that there might be some truth to his cousin's teasing.

"No, but maybe you'd like to jog behind us, while we and our horses enjoy a peaceful gallop," teased Oliver.

"Sure," groaned Kevin. "Got any other great tips?"

"Well, you could also –"

"Don't say it," Kevin warned his cousin, and Oliver laughed.

When all the horses were finally saddled, the four friends guided them past the large paddock and toward the woods.

"Oh no, we're not going to Echo Lake again, are we?" Cathy let Rashid catch up to Diablo and frowned at Ricki. "We rode there all last week, and frankly, I'd like to ride somewhere else for a change. It's getting boring."

"But it's beautiful!" answered Ricki enthusiastically.

"And it's practical in this heat, because we can let the horses go into the water," added Kevin.

"Exactly! So Echo Lake is the perfect place to get this little foal used to going into water," Oliver ended the debate.

Cathy stuck out her tongue at him. "Now you're siding against me, too. That's just great!"

"Hey, what's with you, Cathy? Nothing seems to please you today, or am I just imagining it?" Oliver glanced at her. "I thought we agreed days ago to take Jessie to the lake today."

"Yeah, we did ... but we've taken this route every day for the past week!"

"Then take a different path," Ricki suggested. "You could ride past Mercy Ranch and visit with Carlotta while we go into the water with Jessie. I'm sure she'd be happy to see Rashid. Then we could meet up someplace later."

"No, I want to see how the foal does on her first attempt at bathing, too!" replied Cathy, wrinkling her nose in annoyance.

Kevin shook his head. "I'll say it again; women! They never know what they want!"

"And boys usually add unnecessary comments that they would have been better off keeping to themselves," responded Cathy nastily. Oliver was right. Today just wasn't her day. She sighed loudly.

"Of course, if you don't come with us, you won't find out what my surprise is," cajoled Ricki. For Cathy, there was nothing worse than not satisfying her curiosity.

"It's probably not that big of a deal," she mumbled, but Ricki shook her head meaningfully.

"You'd never guess," she said, beaming at Kevin.

"Now I'm getting really curious about whatever it is you want to show us. You do want to show us something, don't you?"

"More or less, yes. But now that I think about it ..."

Kevin groaned. "Now what? You've changed your mind, right?"

His girlfriend laughed. "No, but I really can't make you wait any longer, although it would have been fun, and it would have made Cathy even grumpier." She pointed toward a narrow path that led between the fields and then intersected with the path they were on. "My surprise has unfolded. Look ... here she comes!"

"Oh, wow, it can't be!" Cathy, her mouth open, stared in the direction Ricki was pointing.

"You weren't expecting *that*, were you?" Ricki's eyes gleamed, as though she had magically conjured up the rider on the tall white horse riding toward them.

"Lily! I can't believe it! She's riding again!" Kevin was grinning as widely as Ricki. "When was she allowed to get in the saddle again? I thought she'd have to wait at least six months."

"That's what the doctors said at first, but apparently her bones healed faster than they expected. At least that's what she told me when she called a while ago." Ricki explained.

"Lillian is your friend who had the bad car accident, isn't she?" asked Oliver.

Cathy nodded. "Right! Her horse, Doc Holliday, was stabled at Ricki's place before the accident. But ever since the accident, since she can't ride, she's had him at the Western ranch. That's where her boyfriend, Josh, stables his horse, Cherish. Josh helped take care of Doc. Anyway, that's why the stall was free for your Miz Lizzy and Jessie."

"People, let's not hang around here and talk. Let's go! Lily's back! Finally, everything is the way it used to be." Ricki let Diablo trot. If Jessie hadn't been along, she would have let her horse gallop toward Lily, but she didn't want to take any chances with the foal. And anyway, after all the time that had passed since Lily had been able to ride, a few more seconds wouldn't make a difference now.

It was hard to say who was happier; Lily, or the friends who had sorely missed riding with her during the past few months.

"You can't imagine how thrilled I am to ride Holli again! Of course, Josh was freaked out when I told him I was going to go riding with you guys today. He was actually afraid that I'd forgotten how to ride and was going to fall." She smiled mischievously. "OK, I was a little unsure of myself for the first fifteen minutes," she admitted, "but then it was just like it had been before the accident. Holli is super easy, and I'm as safe on him as in a rocking chair. There's just one little problem."

"And that is?"

"Josh made me promise that I'd be back at the stable in an hour and a half. Otherwise he's sending out a search party. And you know Josh. If he says he'll do something, he'll do it."

Ricki and Lily laughed, thinking Josh was probably organizing the search-and-rescue team right now. But then Ricki got serious and said to her friend, "I think since it's your first time riding after so long, an hour and a half is probably enough. We both know you'll probably go riding every day from now on, and you can gradually stay out longer and longer."

"That's true. But tell me, where should we go? Honestly, I'd really love to ride to Echo Lake. You wouldn't believe how much I've missed it. The whole time I couldn't ride, I kept thinking about how beautiful it is, and I promised myself that my first ride would be to there."

Ricki gave her a thumbs-up. "Wise choice. We wanted

to ride over there anyway, because Oliver wants to get Jessie used to water."

"But Cathy wanted –"

"I always want to go to Echo Lake. Did I ever say anything else?" Cathy innocently looked from one to the other. "If this is Lily's comeback ride, then there's no discussion. The main thing is that we go riding. At the moment, we're doing more talking than riding. Besides, I sense that my Rashid is like a lit stick of dynamite, about to explode any minute."

"Oh, then let's get going. I don't want to be blamed for causing you to fly through the air like you were shot from a cannon," kidded Lillian. Then she reined in Doc Holliday next to Diablo, and the five of them rode off together.

***

"Come on, sweetie, nothing's going to happen to you," Oliver coaxed the foal into the lake. Her neck strained, getting longer and longer, as she nervously stood in water just above her hooves. It was a new sensation for the little horse, and Jessie was willing to follow him only until the water came up over her knees. That was the extent of her courage.

Kevin, who was standing on the bank with Oliver's Miz Lizzy, laughed himself silly, as Jessie began to splash on the surface of the water with her little hooves, giving his cousin a thorough soaking within minutes.

"Oh, great! This wasn't the plan," sputtered Oliver, after getting another spray of water in his face. "Kevin, maybe it would help if you lead Lizzy part way into the water, so Jessie can see that nothing will happen if she goes in a little farther."

"Okay, wait a minute." Kevin took off his boots and

rolled up his jeans. Then he grabbed Miz Lizzy's lead and walked her into the water.

"Look, now Lizzy's splashing, too." Cathy prodded Ricki happily. "Watch out. Guess what's going to happen!"

"What?" Lillian asked just as Oliver's mare went down on her knees and rolled over in the cool water.

"Noooo! Miz Lizzy! Don't!" shouted Oliver. "Oh, no! My saddle! Kevin! Don't let her –" But it was too late.

A few seconds later the horse got back up onto her legs and shook the water out of her coat while Jessie, frightened and with Oliver holding her on a rope, tried to get to shore.

"Oh, bummer!" With a despairing look, he examined his sopping wet saddle. "What a mess! This is going to take at least a week to dry."

"I didn't know Lizzy loved water so much. Next time we should take off her saddle before letting her go into the water," commented Kevin dryly.

"You think?!" Oliver answered sarcastically. "I would never have thought of that!" He glanced at his filly, who was licking the water dripping from her mother's wet coat.

"Oh, whatever ... it's my own fault. I should have known better." He looked at Kevin, who was as wet as Miz Lizzy, and burst out laughing.

"I guess you won't need a shower tonight!" he joked.

"Well, I've always wanted to wash my hair with water-lily extract," replied Kevin and tried to put his riding boots back on. "Oh, no, trying to get your boots on with wet jeans is impossible."

"Men! Always complaining." Lillian winked at Cathy and Ricki.

"You have a free pass today, Lily. It's just lucky the other two didn't say anything."

"And what if we had?" Ricki taunted. "What would you have done then?"

"Do you really want to know?" He grabbed Sharazan's and Diablo's reins and gave them to Lily.

"Watch this. This is what happens to people who make fun of others!" He picked Ricki up in his arms and ran into the water carrying his girlfriend, who was giggling and struggling to get away.

"Noooo, Kevin, don't!" Ricki laughed and screamed, holding on to him for dear life. But Kevin knew no mercy and dunked her halfway into the water before carrying her back to shore.

"Oh, you maniac! How mean was that?" Ricki protested, but she wasn't really mad at Kevin. "I swear, I will get my revenge. Without mercy!"

"That's okay with me," answered Kevin unconcerned, and retrieved Sharazan's reins from Lily.

"I've missed this so much!" Lillian beamed, shaking her head with delight. "You guys are just the same. I don't want to know what else I've missed while I couldn't ride!"

"Yeah, that's what happens when someone thinks she has to throw herself under a car." Cathy grinned.

Lillian nodded. "Sad but true." She looked at her watch and made a long face. "Darn it, I have to go. If I'm late the alarm bells will go off, and Josh'll send out a search party to look for me."

"How about tomorrow? Are we going to meet again? Same time, same place?" asked Ricki.

"No, I can't tomorrow, but I'll call you as soon as I know what my schedule is." Lillian got back in the saddle and picked up Holli's reins. "I would love for you guys to ride part way with me, but I think I'm going to have to gallop some to make it on time. And that's not good for Jessie yet."

Oliver rubbed the foal behind her ears.

"No, not yet. But wait a few weeks, then we'll be able to keep up."

Cathy mounted as well. "I'll ride with you part of the way," she said. "Rashid needs to work off some steam, or he might not let me ride him at all tomorrow."

"Okay, then I'll see you later at the stable," responded Ricki. "Lily, see you. And ... I am *soooo* glad you can ride again!"

Lily smiled gratefully at her. "My sentiments exactly. So, anyway, see you!"

She waved good-bye to her three friends and rode off with Cathy.

"So now what do we do?" Kevin wanted to know.

Oliver gave it a moment's thought. "Well, since I'm already soaking wet, I think I'm going to try again with Jessie. The worst that can happen is that you guys'll have to wring me out!" He laughed and then grabbed Jessie's halter. "Here we go again. Wish me luck."

***

Carlotta Mancini sat in her office. She had turned the desk chair to face the window. From there she could see almost all of Mercy Ranch, including the riding area and the large paddock near the front of the house.

The ranch horses grazed patiently and peacefully on the rich green meadow, looking like an idyllic herd. Someone observing the animals from afar would never have guessed that almost all of them had recently escaped death. However, on closer examination, one could see the scars and scrapes on their coats caused by the ill treatment from their former owners.

15

Lost in thought, the ranch owner stared out at all she had accomplished and suddenly a deep sadness overcame her.

What will happen to all this when I'm no longer here? I wonder if Mercy Ranch will still exist in twenty or thirty years? she asked herself.

Yesterday she had watched an old video of herself performing in the circus when she was young. As always, she had been struck by the fact that time had passed so rapidly, even though it felt like yesterday when she had galloped around the circus ring doing tricks on her white horse. There had been so many wonderful moments in her life, moments that she would always treasure, and some that she would love to experience again. She shook her head to interrupt her own thoughts.

"Carlotta Mancini, don't go getting sentimental on me. It isn't like you," she scolded herself out loud before she was startled by a knock on the door.

Manuela Martin, a photographer and a good friend, stood in the doorway. With a victorious laugh, she waved the most recent issue of the local paper.

"Hey, boss lady, are you okay? I heard you talking to yourself. Have you read the paper yet?" she asked merrily.

"Hi, Manuela. Everything's fine, except for the fact that you just scared me half to death."

"How so? I don't look that bad, do I?" The photographer laughed.

"Ah, Manuela, you know you're always a sight for these sore eyes," Carlotta replied as she ushered her into the kitchen.

"Well? Have you?"

"Have I what?"

"Have you read the paper, silly."

"No. I haven't had the time."

"Then it's time you did." Manuela laid the paper on the kitchen table and turned the pages until she found what she was looking for.

"Look at this. The editor gave you a whole double page spread. Isn't that great? Sid did a wonderful job, and he integrated your entire interview into the article. It really turned out well."

Curious, Carlotta pulled the paper toward her and skimmed the photos first.

"Your photos are pretty great, too, especially the ones of the horses." She winked at her younger friend. "You could have left out that photo of me, though."

"Nonsense! That photo is terrific. And with this article, if anyone doesn't know you yet, they –"

"Will get to know me!" Carlotta finished the sentence. "I especially want to reach those who still think it's okay to mistreat horses."

"Them, too, of course, but I was thinking of the potential visitors who will come to see you at the open house."

"Do you really think there will be that many visitors?"

Manuela nodded enthusiastically. "Definitely. This article and the photos will make people curious about the person behind the Mercy Ranch initiative."

Carlotta wrinkled her nose and shook her head. "The person, namely me, isn't important. I want to make people aware of suffering horses. If even one person leaves here on that day and decides that in the future he won't turn a blind eye if he witnesses any cruelty to animals, that he'll do something about it, then the whole event will be a success. That's the way you have to look at it, Manuela. Like that, and not any other way."

"Yeah, I know, but that's the long-term effect, so to speak, that the day will offer. It's important that we pique people's interest, and that they come, look everything over and then reflect on what they've seen. And I think with this article that's what we're going to achieve." Manuela smiled. "Now, take your time and read the whole thing."

Carlotta nodded, but she folded the newspaper without looking at it and said, "I don't have any time right now. I have so much to do. If it's all right with you, I'll read this later."

"Sure thing." Manuela looked Carlotta in the eye. "Hey, am I mistaken, or are you not feeling well today? You look pale."

"Don't worry about me." Carlotta winked at her friend and then she got up. "As long as I can stand, I will fight for happy lives for my poor mistreated animals. I promise you that! But for now, my dear Manuela, I'm sorry, but I have to cut our chat short," she said, with noticeable regret in her voice. "Kieran, Hal, and Cheryl are already waiting outside. They want to whitewash the stalls, and before they get more paint in the straw than on the walls, I'd better go and take a look and give them some tarps to spread around."

Manuela laughed and took her coffee mug to the sink. "Okay, boss lady, go ahead. Let your helpers make the ranch shine, so that on the day of the open house, you can make a good impression. I'll come back soon."

"Thanks a lot, Manuela." Carlotta and the photographer walked to the door.

"Hmm, whatever you say. Oops, be careful!" Manuela was just able to grab her friend's arm as Carlotta tripped on the doormat and almost fell. "Are you sure that you're okay?" she asked again.

18

Carlotta looked a little confused, and then squinted up at the sun.

"Strange," she said. "I guess my eyes are getting worse. It looks like I'll have to go to the eye doctor after all."

Manuela let go of her friend's arm. She was concerned.

"I don't like the look of you today."

"Well, I'll only get worse. After all, I'm growing older by the day." Carlotta patted her shoulder. "Don't worry! I'll be all right. See you soon."

With those words, Carlotta picked up one of her crutches, which were parked by the door, and limped over to the stable without looking back. However, she felt Manuela's gaze on her for quite a while.

Chapter 2

Oliver and Kevin already had tended to their horses and taken off for home on their bikes. In the stable Ricki was brushing Diablo for the third time, so that the coat around his saddle and girth area would be smooth and shiny.

Once she was satisfied with her work, she went outside and turned her attention to her saddle. She had wanted to clean and condition it for days, but just as she was about to start her cell phone rang.

"Hey, whoever this is, I don't have time right now!" she said into the phone.

"Hey… Are you stressed out? What's going on?"

"Oh, hi, Kevin, it's you. What's up?"

"You don't have any time, it seems."

"That's because I'm in the process of taking my saddle apart," Ricki explained.

"Why? The big cleanup, with saddle soap?"

"Yup!"

"Darn! I thought you could come out to the ranch and help us paint the stalls."

"I thought you guys were going to do that next week."

"That's what I thought, too, but Kieran and the others don't have time next week, so they decided to start today. They were already at it when I got home."

"Hmmm ... " Ricki thought it over for a minute and tried to decide what she would rather do; clean her saddle or paint walls.

"I'm on my way," she said suddenly and jumped up.

"Great!" Kevin paused a moment before continuing. "Ricki, I have to tell you something when you get here."

"Tell me now. Don't make me wait." Ricki was listening to Kevin with only half an ear; she was running back into the stable to put away her gear.

"Wait a minute, I have to –"

Kevin heard a groan. "Are you listening to me? Ricki! What just happened?"

"I just hit my shin with the bit. Of course, I'm listening to you."

"Yeah, I noticed. What did I just say?"

Ricki hesitated.

"Ahem ... That someone is getting married, but I didn't catch the names. Just a second ..." As she heaved her saddle up onto the wall stand, her cell phone slipped out of her hand. "Darn it! Kevin, are you still there? Kevin?" she called, but the line was dead.

Quickly she tried to call her boyfriend back, but got a busy signal. After several tries, she finally gave up and hurried to return the rags, grease, saddle soap, and brushes to the tack room, while her thoughts were already at the ranch with Kevin.

About two hours later, Ricki jumped off her bike, totally out of breath, in front of the Mercy Ranch stable.

"Uh-oh, it looks like I'm too late," she said right away. "You're almost done!"

Kevin peered out from one of the stalls.

"How come it took you so long? I thought you'd gotten lost. Should I get you a GPS for Christmas?"

Ricki rolled her eyes.

"Ask Jake," she groaned as she thought of her elderly stable hand. "First, I couldn't find him, then, all of a sudden, there he was in the stable, and he thought up a thousand chores for me. He complained about the tack room, because Cathy hadn't hung up Rashid's martingale and because someone forgot to close the container of hoof grease. He yelled at me for putting my saddle soap and gear in the corner. He said, 'Any pigsty gets cleaned up better than our tack room', and told me to get busy cleaning up the whole mess. And, as if that weren't enough, he decided to replace some of the fence posts around the paddock and, of course, I was chosen to be his assistant." Ricki imitated the old man's voice, exaggerating of course, "You have to hold the post straight. Are your eyes crossed? I said straight. Not to the left, not to the right, and, confound it, don't let go of the thing when I'm pounding it with the sledge hammer!"

Cheryl burst out laughing.

"Weren't you afraid he'd hit your hand?" she asked innocently.

"Well, if you had seen the way Jake was swinging the hammer, you'd have pulled your hands away, too." Ricki shook her head, annoyed, but at the same time she began to chuckle. He was just being Jake, and, truthfully, she didn't want him to be any different, even though he really got on her nerves sometimes. After all, it was Jake who had given her Diablo, and because of that she would happily accept his grumbling anytime.

Ricki pretended to roll up her sleeves.

"So, do you have an extra brush? I love to paint."

Kevin looked at her with some doubt.

"Seriously? You want to volunteer? I almost don't recognize you. But now that I know you're not allergic to volunteering, I'll call you when another opportunity comes along."

"Why? Is something happening?"

"It's possible that very soon there will be a lot of renovating going on here," he said mysteriously.

"Come on, Kev, don't be so mysterious. What's going on?" Ricki asked, and the others, overhearing this cryptic conversation, stopped what they were doing to listen.

"Is there something we should know?" asked Hal just as Sean Devlin, Carlotta's farm manager and right-hand man whom she'd hired six months ago, came into the stable to see how the kids were doing.

Kevin grinned broadly and then he pointed over his shoulder back at the man.

"Ask him."

"Sean? Why him?"

"Yeah, why me?" Devlin played dumb, but his gleaming eyes betrayed the fact that something Kevin had said concerned him.

"Come on, Sean, don't keep us in suspense," pleaded Cheryl.

23

Sean glanced at Kevin. "You just couldn't keep the surprise to yourself, could you?" he chided, looking embarrassed.

"Yes I could, up to now, but if I'm supposed to get a new father, then he should tell everyone himself, don't you think?"

Ricki stared in shock at her boyfriend.

Recovering quickly, she playfully punched Kevin on the shoulder.

"You're getting a new father and you're just telling me that now?"

"I mentioned it a little a while ago on the phone, but you were very busy, apparently, throwing your cell phone around."

"What?" For the moment she was unable to follow her boyfriend's train of thought, but then, suddenly, all became crystal clear.

"The wedding that you mentioned ..."

"Aha! I see the light bulb finally went on," responded Kevin lazily.

Sean's smile turned into a hearty laugh.

"So you did spill the beans. I would have been surprised otherwise. But after all, it isn't a secret that your mother and I want to get married."

"Wow, really?" Kieran came out of a stall, with a paint bucket in his hand, and slapped Sean on the back. "That's great, dude. I've been expecting this for a while."

"You have? Why?" Kevin looked confused.

"Well, it was obvious. The way the two of them kept looking all lovey-dovey at each other, it's been clear for a while now."

Cheryl snorted. "Kieran, you're an idiot, but you're right. We all suspected there was romance in the air."

Giving Sean a hug, she added, "But honestly Sean, I'm

24

really happy for you and Caroline, and I'm glad for you, too, Kevin."

"Yeah, totally." Ricki threw her arms around her boyfriend. "You're getting a terrific stepfather!"

Kevin grinned at Sean.

"We'll see ... You can marry my mother, but only if I can get a raise in my allowance," he said with a wink.

"And you, young man, can get a taste of my medicine if your mother isn't worth more to you than a raise in your allowance," replied Sean, laughing.

"Okay, you two can figure this out later." Hal put down his dripping paintbrush. "No raise in your allowance shouldn't be a reason not to have a wedding. Hmmm ... Is it going to be a wedding on horseback?"

"And are you going to live here at the ranch, Sean, or are Kevin and his mother moving into your house?" Cheryl wanted to know.

"So now we're getting back to our topic," Kevin interrupted the barrage of questions from his friends. "Didn't I mention the renovation work a while ago?"

Sean nodded.

"We're going to build an addition to the ranch, where we can have our own space so that we won't get in Carlotta's way when I'm living here as well," explained Sean, and then turned to Hal. "We haven't decided yet whether or not it will be an equestrian wedding."

"Of *course* it will be an equestrian wedding. What else could it be? You ride, Caroline used to raise horses, Kevin rides, you live at Carlotta's horse ranch ... so, hello, there's no other choice but to have a wedding on horseback." Kieran sounded as though the decision was his to make. "So, what do you think, Sean?"

"Well, I don't have anything against a wedding with horses. That would be cool! But don't you think the bride should have a say in this, too?"

Kevin's eyes gleamed and his broad smile lit up his whole face. Ricki realized that she had never seen her boyfriend as happy as he was at this moment.

Quickly her thoughts went over the past, beginning with Kevin's parents' divorce. His father had been really awful back then, to both Kevin and his mother. She was thrilled that Sean, who was so nice, was going to create a new family with Caroline Thomas, who was just as nice, and her Kevin.

"I think the most important thing is that you're going to be happy, whether it's an equestrian wedding or not," she commented.

"We *are* happy!" responded Sean emphatically. Then he pointed at the walls. "So, now that you have something new to talk about, you guys can get back to work and make some progress here. Kevin, you forgot a twenty-inch space back there in the corner."

"That's terrific! I just allowed that guy to marry my mother, and already he's starting to complain about me." Kevin winked at his future stepfather, grabbed his paint roller, and got back to work.

"Ricki, do you want to help? Then get the little brush and the white window paint. You can try your hand at the frames. But please, tape the windows first, or we'll have a mess to clean off the glass afterward." Sean handed her a roll of blue painter's tape.

"I'll be back later to check on you all," he said and started to leave.

"Oh, that's perfect! First you delegate the jobs, and then

you leave. Hey, where are you off to, anyway?" teased Kevin.

"I'm going to flirt a little. People who are getting married are allowed to do that, you know," replied Sean, amused. As he turned around, he almost bumped into Carlotta, who was just coming into the stable.

"Everything okay with you?" he asked softly.

"Yes, of course," the ranch boss said a little too brusquely and kept on going, trying to avoid any more questions.

"And how are you all doing?" she asked the group of young people expansively. "It looks to me as though you're almost finished."

"Yes, just one more wall and a few windows. We'll be done today, no problem." Kieran pointed after Sean. "How long have you known about Sean and Kevin's mother?"

"Oh, about two months," estimated Carlotta.

"What? Then you've known about it longer than I have." Kevin pretended to be upset. "And you didn't say anything."

"Nope."

"That wasn't very nice of you," said Kevin, grinning. "Just for that you have to help me with something. Hal just had a terrific idea about having an equestrian wedding, and I want you to help me persuade my mother and Sean."

Carlotta nodded. "I already had the same idea, but at the end of the day those two have to make the decision themselves. After all, it is *their* wedding."

"That doesn't mean there can't be surprises, does it?" added Kevin and gave Carlotta a peck on the cheek.

***

The next morning Ricki came down to the kitchen in a foul

mood and collapsed wearily onto a chair. She hadn't slept well and, as always when she was plagued by bad dreams, it was better if no one talked to her. In fact, it was even better to leave her alone until she got over it. But for her kid brother, Harold, it was a chance to irritate her even more.

"You look like you swallowed a frog." Harold grinned at her. He had just come in, playing with Ricki's dog, Rosie, and he really didn't care how his big sister was feeling. "Did you forget that you're not supposed to swallow frog princes, just kiss them?" He pulled out a doggie treat from the bag in the cupboard and threw it to Rosie, who caught it in midair and ate it, her tail wagging as she sat on her haunches waiting for more.

"Harry, keep your stupid comments to yourself," replied Ricki, giving him a poisonous look. "And stop stuffing the dog with treats. First of all, too many aren't good for her, and second, you know she gets her treat later in the afternoon. I don't want her to get sick just because you enjoy watching her catch things in the air. Throw her a ball. She'll catch that, too."

"But Rosie doesn't like eating balls."

"You ninny."

"Well, what's going on with you two this morning?" Brigitte Sulai appeared in the doorway and observed her two kids.

"Mom, he keeps getting on my nerves! Could you please tell him to stop feeding Rosie treats every morning? And while you're at it, could you please tell him to leave me alone? I just don't feel like listening to his stupid comments!"

Brigitte looked at her daughter with raised eyebrows.

"Did you get up on the wrong side of the bed today or did you spend half the night talking on the phone?" she asked.

"If you must know, I didn't sleep well. I had a very weird dream and now I have to forget it."

Brigitte had already opened her mouth to scold her daughter for speaking to her in that tone, but instead she asked, "What did you dream about?"

Ricki didn't want to respond. "Oh, just forget about it," was her grumpy reply.

"The way she's acting, Ricki probably dreamed about Kevin cheating on her," laughed Harry, successfully avoiding Ricki, who tried to grab his arm.

"Mom, please, tell him to quit it!"

"Harry, stop that," warned Brigitte. "It's not funny."

"Exactly!" Ricki nodded vehemently. "Harry's never funny. He's just stupid and annoying."

"Ricki, now you stop. Both of you, stop taunting each other!"

"Oh, great, now it's me, huh? And I didn't even do anything!" Ricki got up so abruptly that the chair almost fell over, and she ran outside.

"Ricki, you're impossible," her mother's voice followed her.

"Of course! I'm the one who's impossible! Who else? When it starts like this, the rest of the day's sure to be awful!" the girl angrily grumbled to herself. She slammed the kitchen door a little harder than usual and then ran across to the stable.

"Hello, sweeties. Is everything okay with you, at least?" she asked from the doorway, in Diablo and the other horse's direction. "Be glad that you don't have a little brother. They are really the worst. No, worse than the worst!"

Many wise horse eyes looked over the stall doors at her. Diablo snorted softly. As always, he sensed how his owner was feeling as soon as she entered the stable, and he could tell that she wasn't in a good mood just by the sound of her voice.

He threw his head up and shook his long mane vigorously. He hated it when Ricki was in a bad mood.

"Oh, Diablo, if I didn't have you …" Ricki said and quickly slipped into her horse's stall. Immediately, she leaned against his neck. "Why do mothers always side with younger brothers? Why can't we just have beautiful dreams? And why do I have the feeling that this day is already ruined, even though you're looking at me with so much trust, my sweetheart?" Ricki usually went to her horse first with all her problems and questions. Even though it wasn't possible for him to answer her like a human, she felt as though he understood her better than anyone else.

"How come you're up so early today?" someone asked suddenly, and Ricki jumped.

"Good grief, Jake, you always manage to scare me early in the morning," she said to the elderly stableman, who suddenly appeared standing in front of the stalls.

"No, I don't. During school vacations you're usually still in bed this time of day."

"I couldn't sleep," murmured Ricki, and then she hurried past the old man. "The best thing for tiredness and a bad mood is to go riding, don't you think so, Jake?"

"What? You're in a bad mood, too? Well then, get going before it gets to me, too," he grinned, and went back to work as Ricki left Diablo's stall to get her gear from the tack room. She planned to brush his coat quickly so that she could go riding right away. She looked forward to riding on the open terrain and hoped to free herself from her bad mood.

30

Soon she was mounted and trotting along the narrow path through the meadow, on the way to her favorite path to Echo Lake.

She had ridden along this path frequently in the past few years, mostly with happy but sometimes with sad or desperate thoughts, but there was hardly a time she had not returned with a lighter and happier heart. Today, she hoped that the magic of the lake would make her think pleasanter thoughts, but the closer she came to her favorite place, the more depressed she became, without knowing why.

"Come on, boy. Help me get my mind on other things," she said to Diablo, and gripped his belly a little tighter with her calves to urge him to go faster.

As always, Diablo reacted to the lightest gesture from his rider. Ricki claimed that he almost always knew what she wanted from him before she did. Today Diablo changed from a trot to a gentle gallop as soon as he felt the slight pressure from her thighs.

Weightlessly and in regular beats, the black horse's hooves thundered along the narrow path. Past dense bushes bordering the undergrowth he galloped, constantly trying to avoid missteps that could be dangerous for his rider. He sensed that Ricki wasn't focused today. She sat absentmindedly in the saddle and watched the trees flying past her without really being aware of them. Her eyes were staring straight ahead but she wasn't watching the path.

When Diablo started to slow down and trot again without her guiding him, Ricki seemed to awaken from a trance.

"What's going on?" she asked her horse with some annoyance. "Don't you feel like galloping anymore?" For a fraction of a second she thought about urging Diablo to speed up again, but then she recognized the reason for his slowing and quickly brought him to a standstill. There, where the path disappeared behind the bushes and trees in a slight curve, a horse without its rider came trotting toward them. The reins dragged on the ground and the saddle hung crookedly, causing the stirrups to beat against the horse's belly.

Ricki held her breath. She hoped the animal wouldn't get his front hooves caught in the reins. The consequences of a horse falling could be terrible.

She tried immediately to get an overview of the terrain, hoping she could see the rider who had obviously fallen off, but she couldn't detect any movement in the woods.

"Oh my goodness, that's Sheila!" she burst out. "Sheila ... *Sheila*! Come here, my little one. Come." Coaxing with a comforting voice, Ricki called the horse, who, recognizing the familiar voice, raised her head and pointed her ears.

"Sheila, come," called Ricki again, and as the mare started trotting toward her, Sheila caught sight of the black gelding and greeted Diablo with a soft whinny. Quickly Ricki slid down from the saddle and reached out her hand to the animal.

Sheila snorted boldly, came closer, and then allowed Ricki to grab her reins. Ricki breathed a sigh of relief.

"Where did you leave Cheryl?" asked Ricki, slightly concerned. "You didn't make her fall off, did you?"

Sheila was one of the horses at Mercy Ranch, and Ricki supposed that Cheryl, who was a daily helper there, along with Hal and Kieran, had gone riding on Sheila and had fallen off somewhere. Although Sheila was an extremely gentle and affectionate horse, in open terrain she wasn't

32

always reliable. Every once in a while she would freak out, and then she bucked like a rodeo horse. Cheryl wasn't always able to control her, even though she knew the Black Forest mare's habits extremely well.

Now happy and trusting in the company of those she knew, Sheila nuzzled Ricki's hand before bumping into Diablo, as if to say, "Hey, let's go out on the trail without our riders."

Holding securely to Sheila's reins, Ricki mounted Diablo again and then rode on in the direction from which the horse had come, with Sheila following behind.

"Cheryl? Cheryl, where are you?" she called loudly into the woods. Even after the bend in the path, her friend was nowhere to be seen.

"Cheryl?" Ricki bit her lip. If only she knew where to search! After all, Sheila could have been anywhere when she broke away, and not necessarily in the woods. And if that were true, then Cheryl's whereabouts would remain a mystery.

"Now, if you were Flicka, you would take me directly to your rider," sighed Ricki and regarded Sheila with a side glance, as she recalled the horse in one of her favorite books. "But no, you're just Sheila. What am I going to do with you now? If I take you home, Cheryl will spend hours looking for you and panic if she doesn't find you. But I can't ride around with you for hours and just hope that I find your rider somewhere. I have no idea where you were when you took off."

Sheila trotted contentedly next to Diablo and paid no attention to Ricki's monolog. Unsure of what to do, Ricki kept on riding. She bet that Cheryl was worried sick about her foster horse, and it was easy for Ricki to

33

identify with her. She had been in the same situation once and had searched for Diablo for hours before finding him, thankfully uninjured.

It's probably best if I bring Sheila back to Mercy Ranch, she thought, as she rode along the banks of Echo Lake. Because Cheryl was still missing and Ricki was worried that she might have injured herself in the fall, she didn't even notice how beautiful the lake was that day.

Worried thoughts urged her onward. She hoped that nothing had happened to Cheryl.

When she finally left the woods with the two horses and started down the stony path between the meadow and the field that would lead her to Mercy Ranch, she saw, far in the distance, a slender person limping toward her.

"Hey, can that be Cheryl?" Ricki tightened Diablo's reins and let him trot, and she had to keep urging Sheila to keep up by clicking her tongue.

But it wasn't Cheryl.

"Carlotta, where did you come from? Don't tell me *you* were riding Sheila," she called as she brought the horses to a stop in front of the owner of Mercy Ranch.

"Ricki, what luck that you happened to be around and caught her," said Carlotta, relieved. She took the Black Forest mare's reins from the girl's hand.

"I thought Cheryl had gone riding with Sheila but I was wrong. Are you okay? Did you fall off? Are you hurt?" asked Ricki, visibly upset, her words bursting out of her.

Carlotta waved her worries aside.

"It's nothing," she replied easily. "Maybe old women just shouldn't ride."

"Old women! I can't believe you said that," countered Ricki.

"Well, it's true. Even if I was a good rider once, I just don't have the confidence anymore. Ever since I was crippled in that accident so many years ago, I haven't ridden much."

"Don't be silly. As though you could ever forget how to ride. Maybe someone else, but not you. Never. Tell me what really happened."

"I can't say exactly." Carlotta looked at Sheila questioningly, as though she could perhaps answer Ricki's question better. "I was riding somewhere between the cornfields, and I must not have been paying attention for a moment. I was probably thinking about something else. Just then a jackrabbit jumped up between the rows of corn and landed right in front of Sheila's hooves. She was naturally scared to death and she jumped to the side and bolted. And I fell off, of course."

Carlotta looked at Ricki as she adjusted Sheila's saddle and tightened the girth. She didn't tell her that during the ride she had suddenly blacked out and that had been the cause of her fall. "I'm glad nothing happened to our girl. Thanks a lot, Ricki. I owe you."

"You don't owe me a thing," responded Ricki. "I'm just so glad that nothing happened to either of you." Then she waited until the older woman was back in the saddle. "It's really unusual to see you riding."

"Yes, I know."

"How come you went riding today, of all days? Isn't your car working?"

"No, that's not it. I just felt like going riding on this lovely morning."

"And you happened to choose Sheila because she's always so stubborn."

Carlotta nodded. "Exactly. But which horse should I have ridden, in your opinion? Old Jonah, with his worn-out joints? Or Jam, because he's so small and it's not so far to fall? Or Hadrian?"

"At least Hadrian wouldn't have thrown you."

"Maybe. But I think it was all my fault. I just wasn't paying attention. I was thinking about other things."

For a while they rode silently next to each other.

Ricki glanced at Carlotta from the corner of her eye.

The older woman kept rubbing her forehead.

"Did you hit your head when you fell?"

"No. I've been having a lot of headaches recently, but I'm sure it'll pass. I think I'm a little stressed. Maybe after the open house I'll take a few days vacation."

"You, on vacation? You know that will never happen. You wouldn't be able to last three days away from the ranch," Ricki said.

Carlotta grinned. "You might be right. Well, I think a little riding wouldn't be amiss, especially if I don't end up staring at the underside of a horse's belly."

They continued riding next to one another without talking, both lost in their own thoughts.

Every once in a while Ricki glanced over at Carlotta. She noticed that the ranch owner was not quite her usual self, but doubted that it was due to being thrown by Sheila.

"I'm going to come by again this afternoon," she said when they had reached the fork in the path where they would separate.

"You want to do the tack room, don't you?"

Ricki nodded.

"You kids really did a wonderful painting job yesterday," said Carlotta, full of gratitude for Ricki and her friends. "The stable and stalls have never looked so good."

"I think the horses like it, too," responded Ricki, beaming with pride. "Take care of yourself, Carlotta," she called to the older woman.

"Don't worry, I've never been thrown twice on one ride before. See you later," answered Carlotta, winking. She waved happily to Ricki, and when the girl and Diablo had disappeared behind the bushes Carlotta urged Sheila into a trot. It was time to get home. She had an appointment that she didn't want to miss.

Chapter 3

"Why can't I shake the feeling that everyone is worried about me?" Carlotta asked Sean, who had picked her up from the doctor's office. "Just because I fell off a horse and my eyesight has gotten a little worse, everyone's acting as though I'm gravely ill."

Sean took a deep breath before he answered, "That's not true; you're just imagining it."

"Hmm, if you say so ..."

"Maybe you should take a few days off and go some-where and just relax."

"Are you trying to get rid of me?" Carlotta asked with a coy smile. "Unfortunately, that's impossible. There's so much to do before the open house, not to mention all the paperwork I'd still have to take care of before I could even think about getting away for a few days."

"Just stop that, Carlotta. Your health is much more

important than the office or the open house. We could easily postpone the event."

"No, we will not," Carlotta shot back decisively. "That day has been set and it's going to stay that way. Think about that article in the newspaper. It wouldn't be right to have announced the event and then cancel it. No, no, we're not going to do that."

Sean, who was very fond of his boss, furrowed his brow in concern. "What did the doctor say, exactly?"

"We'll talk about it another time."

"Aha!" He looked down at Carlotta. "Am I correct in thinking that he recommended a vacation?"

"I'm not answering without my lawyer! ... Well, you're right, more or less. Please Sean, drive me home now. I have a lot to do today!"

***

Late that afternoon, Ricki and Kevin entered the Sulai stable holding hands. Cathy was waiting for them, apparently a little miffed.

"Hey, what took you so long? I thought we were going riding today."

"Sorry, Cathy, but, honestly, I'm too tired," Ricki begged off, stifling a yawn. "We were at Mercy Ranch and cleaned up the entire tack room. Anyway, I already went riding this morning with Diablo."

"That's just fabulous. And I waited for you. If I'd known earlier, I would have taken Rashid riding on my own. Or I would have gone with you to the ranch and helped. Anyway, you two worked at Carlotta's yesterday. How come nobody ever tells me anything?"

"Oh, Cathy, don't pout," Ricki put her arm around her friend's shoulder affectionately. "Yesterday just turned out like that, I didn't plan it that way. And today ... well, come on, don't make such a big deal out of it. Besides, if you don't cheer up, I won't tell you the amazing news," cajoled Ricki. She glanced at Kevin. "Can I tell her or do you want to?"

The boy laughed. "Sure, go ahead."

"Humph!" Cathy grunted, still a little peeved, although she looked at the two of them with obvious curiosity.

"Well, you're not going to believe this, but Kevin's mother is getting married again. And guess to whom."

"Nooo, really?"

Kevin nodded, beaming.

"And to whom? I have no idea. Jake?" she giggled. "I don't know anyone else."

"I think I'm over the age limit to get married," broke in the old stableman, who, once again had unexpectedly and silently appeared.

"Oh, Jake, you should never say never. If you suddenly fall in love with someone, she isn't going to ask your age," Ricki said, laughing.

"Maybe not, but she'll be able to tell just by looking at me," grumbled Jake, but he, too, was all ears, waiting for Ricki's answer.

"The lucky man is Sean Devlin."

"No way!"

"Yes, way."

"That is so cool." Cathy rolled her eyes romantically. "I'm so happy for them. This is absolutely, totally amazing. So, when is it?"

"The wedding?" Kevin hesitated, thought it over, and then shrugged his shoulders. "I have no idea. Now that I think about it, the two lovebirds haven't said anything yet,

40

so they probably haven't decided when. I'm pretty sure it'll be soon, though."

"How do you know? Maybe they're the kind that are engaged longer than they're married," commented Ricki. Kevin grinned and shook his head.

"They aren't like that," he replied.

"And what makes you so sure?" Ricki asked again.

"Uh ... how should I say this? The thing is, I'm going to have a baby brother ... or sister."

"What did you say?" Ricki was stunned by this announcement and plopped down onto a bale of straw lying in the corridor. For a minute, she was tempted to tell Kevin about all the disadvantages of having a younger sibling, but she decided to let it go. After all, her boyfriend had always wanted a little brother or sister, and his greatest wish was going to come true.

"Well, not immediately," explained Kevin, "but when Mom and Sean told me about getting married, they also said that they plan to have kids."

"That's ... that's ... fabulous!" she said then, letting him know she was really happy for him. After all, not every younger sibling was as bratty as her brother Harry.

"Yeah, it is. Mom always wanted to have more kids, but my dad didn't. And then there was the divorce ..."

Cathy grabbed Kevin by the shirt collar and pulled him toward her. "Come here, you; I want to give you a hug. This is double-dynamite news. You're going to have a whole new family. I'm so happy for you, Kev."

Ricki turned her gaze on Diablo, who was standing contentedly in his stall. "I think I'd like to take a little ride after all. I need to get used to this news."

"Why do *you* have to get used to it?" he asked. "It

41

doesn't have anything to do with you ... Well, maybe just a little."

"A little is enough," Cathy hurried to agree with her girlfriend. "The main thing is we're going riding today. And meanwhile, Kevin, you can fill us in on all the details."

***

"Oh, wow, I really envy you," commented Cathy a little while later, on their ride. She gave Kevin a long look. "I've always wanted a brother or sister, too, but my mother thinks she has enough to do with just me."

"She's probably right about that," joked Ricki.

"Humph! Agreeing with my mother – that's a low blow. Now my best friend is turning against me." Cathy grinned, and, in response, Ricki stuck her tongue out at her.

"That's just the way I am," she replied before turning to Kevin and beaming. "I think it's terrific that your mother is marrying Sean. He's so nice. The two of them suit each other really well."

"How can you know that? I mean, up to now, no one even knew they were a couple."

"That's not exactly true," Ricki pointed out, guiding Diablo around a fallen branch. "Carlotta knew, and Kieran said he and the other volunteers at the ranch noticed they only had eyes for each other. Anyhow, it doesn't matter. But now that I know, I think it's –"

"Me, too," Cathy chimed in, before her girlfriend could finish her sentence.

"Well, the main thing is that you two agree," laughed Kevin.

Just then, Cathy loosened the reins, bent down over Rashid's neck, and let her arms hang loosely over his shoulders as they continued walking astride their horses.

"Is that your new riding style?" he asked.

"No, but it's really comfortable." Suddenly she sat up and pulled on the reins. "Stop, Rashid. Stand still." Then she jumped down from the saddle.

Ricki and Kevin looked at each other in surprise.

"What's the matter? Did you decide to walk home?"

But Cathy didn't answer. She pulled Rashid two steps forward and then bent down and picked something up. "Look what I found," she called out and waved her arm.

"It's impossible to see what it is with you waving your arm like that. What is it?" Curious, Ricki and Kevin rode up to her.

"A locket." Cathy looked at it intensely. "I like it." She hung it around her neck.

"You have to bring it to the town's lost and found. Whoever lost it is probably looking for it."

"Of course, I will. But until we get home, it'll be better if I wear it. We don't want it to get lost again." She hurried back into the saddle.

"Just a minute, let me see it." Ricki leaned over to her friend. "You can forget about the lost and found. I know whose this is."

"Really? Who?"

"It's Carlotta's."

Cathy's eyes got huge. "What makes you think that? How did it get here in the first place? Carlotta doesn't go walking in the woods."

"You can open it up. Look inside. Her daughter's picture is in there."

"What daughter?" Cathy and Kevin looked at Ricki with amazement. "Carlotta has a daughter? I didn't know that."

"She had one, but she died of cancer years ago. As far as I know, she wasn't any older than we are now."

43

"Wow, another piece of mind-blowing news. And how do you know all this?" asked Cathy, as she opened the locket and saw the smiling dark eyes of a young girl who looked just like Carlotta.

"Mom told me a while ago. I thought I'd already told you."

"No, you didn't. But if that's true, then Carlotta will be very glad to get this back. But we still don't know how it got here."

Ricki was trying to decide whether to tell her friends about Carlotta's fall, but she decided to keep it to herself. If Carlotta had wanted them to know, she would have told them herself. So, Ricki just shrugged her shoulders.

"I don't have a clue. Maybe she went for a walk around here."

Kevin snorted loudly. "Carlotta and a walk in the woods: that's two worlds colliding. She never has any free time. And besides, have you ever known Carlotta to walk any distance without her crutches, or at least her cane?"

"Then you'll have to ask her, or else this mystery will never be solved," said Ricki, melodramatically. "But I don't think she owes you any explanation about what she does in her free time."

"That's true. It doesn't matter anyway. Let's get going."

"Good idea!"

"Let's ride over to the Western ranch," suggested Kevin. "Maybe we'll run into Lillian and Josh. Did you hear Carlotta say that Josh and his friends were going to put on an exhibition at the open house?"

"Once again, Kevin knows more than the rest of us," grinned Cathy. "There are advantages to living at Mercy Ranch and learning everything first hand."

"Okay, then let's go. I haven't seen the Western riders in a while," responded Ricki. And they turned their horses toward the Western stables.

When they arrived, a good half an hour later, they couldn't believe their eyes.

"Hey, is that really Lillian sitting over there on Holli?" asked Kevin, amazed.

"Looks like it. I can't believe it." Cathy stared with huge eyes.

"Didn't she say that she would never ride Western style?"

"She definitely did."

When the three of them were close enough, Kevin announced, "That is the coolest Western saddle I've ever seen. Hey, Lily, where did you get that? Did Josh finally talk you into riding Western?"

Lillian looked over at her friends, then pushed a strand of hair out of her overheated face and waved.

"Hey! Well, if you board you horse at this ranch, then you have to know something about riding Western," she laughed. "But Holli, my gentle giant, can't compete with these small, agile Western horses anyway."

"That's utter nonsense," interrupted Josh, suddenly appearing at Holli's other side. "It's just a question of training. And considering you've only tried it four times, you're both really good. He patted Holli's flank, then walked over to the visitors. "Hi, you guys. Everything okay with you three? We haven't seen you in a while. I wondered what had become of you."

"Yeah, sorry," Ricki apologized for them. "But we've been busy, too. We've been at Mercy Ranch almost every day, helping to prepare for the big event."

Josh nodded. "It's next weekend, isn't it?"

"You flake! You're supposed to give an exhibition, and you don't even know when it is," chided Kevin.

"I just wanted to make sure." Then Josh turned to Lillian. "Listen, sweetheart, that's enough for today. Your doctor said you shouldn't overdo it."

His girlfriend rolled her eyes and sighed.

"Yes, sir, Doctor Joshua. I know." She started to dismount.

"Wait, I'll help you," called Josh. And he went to her and lifted her gently down from the saddle.

"I can do it by myself," she said, embarrassed, but anyone could see that she enjoyed Josh taking such good care of her.

"How sweet." Ricki turned to Kevin and looked at him wide-eyed. "You could help me down, too."

"Anything else?"

"Nope, that's about it."

Kevin made little circles with his finger near his temple to show he thought she was nuts, and Ricki shrugged.

"Well, it was worth a try." She slid down from her saddle and led Diablo to the paddock fence.

Lillian took Holli back to his stall, and right afterward Josh appeared with his pinto, Cherish, followed by some of his friends and their horses. They wanted to do a little more rehearsing for their exhibition at Mercy Ranch.

"Charon always fascinates me, every time I see him," commented Ricki glancing at the beautiful black-and-white piebald that belonged to Lex, a vet student, who rode into the paddock behind Josh.

Kevin made a sour face.

"As long as Lex doesn't fascinate you, I can deal with your fascination with his horse."

"Oh, Kevin, don't start that again. Lex is just a nice guy, nothing more." Ricki hated it when Kevin got jealous for no reason, and she decided to not let his comments get to her.

All of a sudden they heard the familiar sound of Carlotta's old Mercedes.

"Huh? What's she doing here?" The kids all looked over at the owner of Mercy Ranch in expectation.

"I was just in the neighborhood," Carlotta said, getting out of the car using her crutches. She looked curiously at Josh and the other Western riders as they performed a very good Western-style equestrian show.

"That's wonderful. You should perform in public. You're very good," she shouted to Josh and waved at him encouragingly.

"Open house at Mercy Ranch is enough publicity for us," responded Lillian's boyfriend.

"What do you mean by that?" Carlotta's asked, an expression of bewilderment on her face.

"What do you mean, 'What do you mean?'" Josh asked, just as bewildered.

"I mean about an open house. What does that mean? I don't understand what you're telling me." Carlotta stared at him with wide eyes and shook her head as if she were in a fog.

"I thought we'd discussed that we were going to put on an exhibition at your open house." Josh was somewhat unsettled by Carlotta's forgetting such an important event. "Or has something changed about that?" he wanted to know.

Carlotta glanced at the various Western riders, their faces showing their confusion, and she didn't seem to understand what was going on. She couldn't even remember why she'd come over, but to cover her confusion she smiled.

47

"Yes, right ... I ... I guess I forgot." Slowly she turned and went back to her car.

When she had driven off, the kids looked at one another, a little unsure of what had just happened.

"What was that?" asked Ricki.

"I have no idea," replied Josh. "But if you ask me, there's something wrong with Carlotta."

***

The following days flew by.

The kids had worked hard to make Mercy Ranch more attractive for the open house and thought of many ways to make the event more exciting. The time had come to take care of the final preparations.

Ricki had scheduled to take her daily ride for the last few days with Kevin, so they could help the other kids with last-minute details.

Carlotta was everywhere. She gave good tips and advice here and there, but more and more, she retreated to her office, where the pile of paperwork on her desk was slowly decreasing. Nevertheless, the kids had the feeling that she kept putting off her work to be alone. Her strange behavior at the Western ranch was quickly forgotten, but when Cathy remembered the locket and went to give it back to Carlotta, she sensed that the woman couldn't remember ever having such a piece of jewelry, nor did she seem to know how it had come to be in the woods.

"She's acting so strangely. It seems to me that sometimes she's totally confused," Cathy commented later to her friends.

"Totally overworked, I'd say," guessed Kieran. "When the open house is over, she has to go away for a few days of R and R. We don't want her to collapse."

48

The kids nodded in agreement and decided to speak to Sean about it. After all, he was almost the only one who had any influence on her, and could possibly persuade her to leave the ranch for a few days to relax. Today, however, one day before the event, there was no way anyone could relax. There was still so much to do and everyone was trying to do his or her best to make the open house a huge success.

Kevin's mother was up and in the kitchen early on the last day, preparing dough and batter, fillings and frostings to make the cakes, pies, and pastries that would be served as refreshments.

"What are you going to do if it rains, contrary to all of the forecasts, and the turnout is bad?" asked Sean, embracing his future wife. She couldn't playfully fend him off because her hands were covered in flour.

"What do you think?" asked Lillian, who had volunteered to help Kevin's mother with all the kitchen work. "You'll have to turn into a cake monster, devouring everything in sight, and probably gaining at least twenty pounds in a week!"

Sean groaned. "Twenty pounds? And that's in addition to all the weight I'll gain in the next few years, because I can't say no to Caroline's unbeatable cooking."

"Exactly!" You'll turn into a real marrel." Lillian grinned and held out a freshly baked cupcake for him to try.

Without thinking, Sean reached for it. "A marrel? What in the world is a marrel?"

"A cross between a man and a barrel. What else?" Ricki said, poking her head in the kitchen door. "Has anyone seen Carlotta?"

"No. She's probably in her office. What do you want

her for? Maybe I can help you," Sean offered, hurriedly swallowing the baked treat. "Marrel," he grumbled softly. "That's a good one."

"She's not in her office." Ricki slipped past Caroline and reached for a cupcake herself.

"Hey, if everyone comes by and tries out my cupcakes we'll never finish baking," Lillian complained, but Caroline just laughed.

"It's fine, if everyone likes them. We made so many, it won't matter if some are eaten a little early."

"There, see!" Ricki smiled at her girlfriend, and then took a bite.

"Mmmm! Yummy. You did good, Lily. By the way, it's great that you're here," she said, "and Josh coming tomorrow with the Western riders to give an exhibition is pretty terrific, too."

Lillian nodded. "Yeah, Carlotta thought it was a good idea not only to show what abuses horses are suffering but also the terrific things you can train them to do."

"What do you want Carlotta for?" asked Sean again.

"Oh, yeah, right ... I want to ask her if Kevin and I can stable Sharazan and Diablo here tonight. If we can, then we won't have to ride back to my place later on. I could stay here at the ranch with Kevin and Caroline and then I could help out early tomorrow morning. If we have to ride back with the horses then we'll lose two hours at least until we get back here, and there's still so much to do. Manuela is going to deliver two party tents in a little while, the tables have to be cleaned and set up, and we want to groom all the horses today so that we'll be done before the official opening tomorrow, and –"

Sean laughed. His laugh was always warm, jovial, and

heartfelt. "Stop before I have a nervous breakdown and run off just from hearing everything that's left to do."

"Yeah, and that's why I want to ask Carlotta if –"

"Listen, I don't think there's a problem with that. The three guest stalls are still empty, so I'm sure Sharazan and Diablo can stay here overnight. But still, see if you can find Carlotta. And if you do find her, let me know, okay? I have a few things I want to discuss with her."

"Okay," replied Ricki, and left to go looking for the owner of the ranch. However, she was nowhere in the house.

Maybe she's in the stable, Ricki thought, taking the three front steps of the house in one jump. But instead of going directly into the stable, she ran over to the paddock, where her Diablo and Kevin's Sharazan were dozing in the warm summer sun with the two old-timers, Hadrian and Jonah.

"You guys have a great life," Ricki called to the horses as she entered the meadow. "All you have to do is stand around and enjoy the sun and eat. I really envy you." She threw her arms around her black horse and stroked him, making the gelding snort with pleasure.

But the teenager immediately wrinkled her nose in disgust. She noticed that her horse had managed – once again – to roll in manure, so that he was enveloped by an extremely unpleasant odor and his belly was covered with greenish slime.

"Diablo, you piglet! Now I have to wash you all over again, to keep you from chasing all the visitors away with your hideous smell. Couldn't you be careful for once?" she scolded him loudly. But Diablo just nuzzled her shoulder affectionately, completely unimpressed.

Don't be so upset, his eyes seemed to say. *We horses do this kind of thing, and that's all there is to it.*

"As though I didn't have enough to do," whined Ricki, but she gave her four-legged sweetheart a kiss on his smooth muzzle.

Just then, Manuela and her daughter, Carla, arrived, with the two party tents in a little trailer attached to the back of their car.

Carla jumped out of the car and threw her arms around Ricki enthusiastically.

"Hey there. How are you? I haven't seen you in ages."

Ricki was equally happy to see her old friend from the Avalon Riding Academy.

"I know. Weren't you going to visit us with Rocco? How is your adorable little horse? Everything okay?"

Carla grinned. "Of course. Rocco is just fine. And before you ask, yes, Mom's darling Shine is fine, too, and so is Comet. Michelle is doing really well with him in the paddock. I think we'll be ready to try our first trail ride soon."

"Terrific! And after such a short time. I never would have believed it." Ricki was impressed. She remembered that Michelle had been afraid of horses the first time she had come to Mercy Ranch. But then she had fallen in love with Comet, the little gelding, and was thrilled to receive the horse from her parents as a present. Carlotta had been glad to give the poor animal, which had been mistreated by a handler, to a loving family. Under the expert supervision of Manuela and Carla, at their ranch where Comet was boarded, Michelle and Comet had gotten back their self-esteem. It was a real pleasure to hear about their progress.

Manuela had gotten out of the car too and now she shook hands with Ricki.

"Hi, Ricki. Where's Carlotta? Do you know where these two tents are supposed to be set up?" Then she glanced up at the sky.

"We probably won't need them anyway. It doesn't look anything like rain, but they're good for protection against the sun as well," she laughed. "So, where's the boss lady?"

Ricki shrugged her shoulders.

"I'm looking for her myself," she said, "and she can't be far. Her car is where it always is and all of the horses are here, so she hasn't gone driving or riding."

"Carlotta going riding? That would really be something new!" Carla burst out, but before Ricki could reply, Hal and Kieran came out of the stable.

"Back there on the second paddock," called out Kieran and waved his arms dramatically. However, Manuela and the two girls just looked at him as if he were speaking Martian.

"The tents! They're supposed to go there. Carlotta told us this morning," he explained quickly.

"Oh, okay. Then I'll drive over there." Manuela nodded, getting back in her car as the kids ran behind her.

"We might as well put them up right now. When we're finished, we have to prepare the games for the kids," Hal reminded the others.

"And we have to get the props ready for the Western exhibition," added Kieran.

"And we have to cover the tables with cloths so they look nicer," Ricki added to the growing list.

"And we still have more to do," Hal added.

"I never thought there'd be so much preparation," sighed Ricki.

Carla laughed. "Yeah, and in a sense, it's all your fault.

Who had the great idea, a few weeks ago, to have an open house at Mercy Ranch?"

"At the time I was totally bored. Otherwise, I can't explain what made me suggest this," admitted Ricki.

"Boredom? What's that?" Kieran gave Ricki a little poke in the ribs. "Still, once you start something, you have to finish it."

"Naturally. And I still think it's a great idea," Ricki defended herself. "Honestly, though, I'll be glad when everything is ready and people arrive here tomorrow, and even happier tomorrow night when everything is over and everyone is happy."

"Okay, but until tomorrow night, there are still ..." Hal looked at his watch, "... still about twenty-eight hours to go. That means we have no time to stand around and talk, if we're going to be finished in time."

Together the kids ran to the paddock where the tents were to be erected. There they listened to Manuela instruct them on how to stretch out the parts of the tents, while the horses on the neighboring paddock quickly galloped away upon sighting the large poles and enormous white, scary cloth panels.

By the time the kids were pushing the first corner poles through the sides of the tents, Ricki had long forgotten that she was supposed to be looking for Carlotta so she could tell Sean where to find her.

***

An hour and a half later, the party tents were finally up.

"That looks terrific." Caroline and Lillian leaned out of the kitchen window and gave their thumbs-up.

Manuela and Carla waved good-bye to them as they walked to their car. They had to get back home to the work awaiting them at their own stable.

"Actually, you could just leave them there for your wedding, couldn't you?" Lillian beamed at Kevin's mother.

"Don't tell me; everyone knows?" she asked laughing.

"Of course."

"We haven't even picked a date."

"Oh, you can't get out of it now," responded Lillian, and then she glanced at her watch. "I think it's almost time for me to leave. Josh will be here any minute to pick me up."

"Well, then get going. Thanks so much for your help, Lillian. Without you, I would never have been able to get everything done." Caroline smiled and gave her a hug. "See you tomorrow."

"You bet. See you then." Lillian got up and walked slowly out of the kitchen. She still moved rather cautiously and would probably continue to do so for quite a while yet. After several bone-mending operations, it would take some time before she felt normal when she walked.

Just as Lillian was about to open the front door, Sean came storming up the steps and ran past her, almost knocking her over as he flew into the kitchen. He seemed not to see her.

"Oh, hi, Sean. I wanted to say good-bye to you, but it doesn't matter that you didn't even notice me." Lillian murmured with a glance at the kitchen door. "Good grief, I never realized that adults in love were just as crazy as teenagers." Shaking her head, she left the house and sat down on the front steps to wait for Josh.

Sean, on the other hand, was saying to Caroline at the same moment, "I can't find Carlotta."

Kevin's mother looked up. The worry on her face was unmistakable.

"Where have you looked? She *has* to be here."

"I've looked everywhere. She's just not here."

"That's impossible!"

"I'm really worried about her," Sean confessed. "Yesterday she wanted to order some feed, but she couldn't remember the name of the delivery company. I gave her the number and when she finally had the mill on the line she couldn't remember what she wanted to order."

Caroline turned pale. "You didn't tell me that."

"With all that's going on here, I didn't want to worry you."

"Worry me? I'm already worried. I've noticed how forgetful she's been lately, too."

Caroline grabbed Sean's hand and pulled him along. "Come on. We're going to look everywhere systematically until we find her. And when we do, we're not going to let her out of our sight. Once tomorrow is over, I'm going to have a talk with her and make sure that she goes to the doctor and gets examined. Her behavior is just not normal."

"But she already was at the doctor."

"When?" Caroline stopped and stared at Sean, as the two of them were searching the house for Carlotta.

"It was a while ago."

"Sean, don't make me beg for every word. What did the doctor say?"

Sean shook his head.

"I don't know. She didn't tell me."

Chapter 4

"I am *so* exhausted," Ricki said to Kevin that evening as they headed back to the ranch house. "You could have helped us set up the tents. Where were you while we were doing that, anyway?"

"Cheryl and I were cleaning out the stalls and putting down fresh straw. For some reason, Sean was nowhere to be found and I saw Carlotta only once all day. Do you know if she's home?"

Ricki slapped her forehead in annoyance, suddenly remembering, "Oh, no, I completely forgot that Sean asked me to look for her. Oh, well, she's probably turned up by now. Man, Kevin, I'm dead tired and I just want to go to sleep, but it's too early for that. What do you want to do now?"

"First, have dinner, and then after, maybe we can go riding for a while."

"Riding? Are you crazy? I'd fall right out of the saddle. No, I was thinking more like watching television or something easy like that."

Kevin put his arm around his girlfriend. "Sorry, honey bug, television is out ... our satellite connection is down."

"You're not serious, are you?" groaned Ricki. "How do you stand it with no TV?"

"Oh, you can get used to anything. There's nothing good on TV anyway."

Changing the subject, Kevin asked, "Hey, how come Cathy didn't come today? Didn't she want to help?"

"Yeah, she did. Didn't I tell you that she called me last night?"

Kevin shook his head.

"I must have forgotten. She slipped on the carpet at home and sprained her ankle. Now she can't stand on it," said Ricki.

"That's tough."

"It sure is."

Arm in arm they went into Carlotta's kitchen, which smelled as wonderful as a restaurant. Caroline was standing at the stove preparing ham salad for all the people who had helped that day.

"It's almost ready," she mumbled, seeing Kevin's hungry glance. "You two could set the table."

But Kevin sensed something in his mother's tone of voice that made him feel uneasy. "Okay ... Hey, is anything wrong?"

"No, not that I know of," replied Caroline.

"Well, that's good, Mom, because it's going to be a great event tomorrow. I just hope that lots of people come, or else I'm going to be really annoyed," commented Kevin. "We've been working so hard."

"Manuela has been doing a lot of publicity in the last few weeks, so I think it'll be a success. Still, I'll be glad when tomorrow night comes and it's over." Caroline put a large bowl of ham salad, a platter of lettuce and tomatoes, baskets of buns and potato chips, and two big pitchers of lemonade on the table. "Please, go call the others, and when you're finished I'd appreciate it if you would clear the table."

"Aren't you going to eat with us?"

Caroline shook her head.

"No. I'm not hungry now; just a little tired. I've put aside some food for Carlotta and Sean. That means you kids can eat everything on the table." She looked sleepily at her son before leaving the room. Sean hadn't found Carlotta yet and was still out searching for her. They had agreed that she wouldn't say anything to the kids yet because they didn't want them to worry, but if Carlotta wasn't found soon, then the kids would have to be told so they could help look for her.

Ricki turned to her boyfriend.

"What's wrong with your mother?"

"No idea, but I'm not going to think about it until I have something to eat. I'm starving."

"When aren't you starving?" asked Ricki, laughing, and then she went outside quickly to get the other kids.

***

"Nothing." Sean stood before Caroline completely at a loss. "It's as though she's disappeared from the face of the earth. It's just impossible, isn't it?"

"I've looked for her for two hours and I haven't found her, either. I think we'd better get the kids to help us. If Carlotta really is a little confused then she could be

59

anywhere. She was probably gone for hours before we even realized she was missing. I'd like to call the police and get their help."

"I don't think that would help. After all, she's an adult, who up to a little while ago was completely fine. They probably wouldn't start a search for her until she's been gone forty-eight hours."

"Okay, then I'll get the kids together and we'll start looking again, for the fourth time." Caroline ran off toward the kitchen.

***

Sad and upset, the kids were standing close together listening to Sean. Their faces were drawn and pale.

"Carlotta has disappeared ... She's been having problems thinking logically lately ... I have no idea where she is ..." Only the most important phrases remained in Ricki's head.

"So, in short, we have the best chance of finding Carlotta if we all look for her together," Sean was saying.

"Does this have anything to do with her falling off Sheila?" Ricki asked, worry showing all over her face.

"What? She went riding on Sheila?" Cheryl asked in surprised. However, instead of answering her, Ricki focused her attention on Sean.

"I don't think so," he said. "She was a little mixed up before that."

"Come on, people, hurry up. We can talk about what might have happened later. Let's get going. We don't want to lose any more time. After all, we don't even know if Carlotta might need our help," urged Caroline. "And it'll be getting dark soon."

"I'm taking Gandalf with me. Maybe he can find her," Kevin hoped. He whistled for his dog.

"That's a good idea. I'll get Carlotta's Happy and we'll go together." Kieran ran to the house to get the dog leash.

Ricki and Cheryl looked at one another in silent agreement.

"We'll ride," they said almost simultaneously. "Carlotta could be anywhere, and it might be good if we're on horseback. We can cover a lot more territory than we could on foot."

Sean nodded.

"Good. Then Hal can come with me," he said.

"And I'm –" began Caroline, but Sean interrupted her.

"Going to stay put in case someone calls," he ended her sentence. "She might show up back home, and then you can get in touch with us. There's no sense in all of us leaving, and, anyway, you've been on your feet enough today. Get some rest."

Caroline sighed. "All right," she agreed. "I have all of your cell phone numbers in the house. If anything happens, I'll call."

"Okay, then let's quickly discuss who's going to search where, and then we'll get going."

***

Manuela Martin had gone on a wonderful ride with Carla and she was just brushing her horse, Shine, as Carla came running into the stable with her mother's cell phone.

"It's for you, Mom," she called and held the phone out to her.

"Who is it?" asked Manuela.

"Carlotta, but she seems strange," whispered Carla, putting her hand over the receiver.

With an unsettled look on her face, the photographer took the phone, cleared her throat, and then answered as she always did when her friend was on the line.

61

"IRS ..."

For a moment there was silence, and then Carlotta responded, sounding confused, "Oh, excuse me, I have the wrong number," and hung up.

"No, wait, I ..." Bewildered, Manuela looked at the phone in her hand. "What's going on? She knows I always say that!"

"I told you she was acting strange."

Manuela thought for a moment. "What's even stranger is the fact that she hung up, considering the fact that you'd already answered the phone with your name, and she has to know that I'm the only one you'd give the phone to. Strange ... really strange! I'm going to call her back."

Carla looked at the driveway over her mother's shoulder. "You don't need to. Here she comes."

"What?" Manuela whirled around. "Why are you on foot? Did you get a flat tire? And why did you call when you were almost here anyway?" she called out.

Carlotta stood still and looked at Manuela. Her eyes were wide open and looked glazed and disoriented.

"Please, excuse me, but I think I'm lost. I'm looking for Manuela Martin. She lives around here somewhere."

Manuela and Carla exchanged a brief glance.

"What in the world ...?"

"I'm pretty sure I'm on the right road, but now I just can't figure out where I am. I haven't been to her house in a long time."

Manuela beamed at her. She thought Carlotta was joking, and decided to play along with the game.

"May I offer you a cup of coffee? Then we can try to figure out together where Mrs. Martin lives. I'm fairly certain that we can find the right house."

Carla's eyes asked unspoken questions: *Mom, what's going on? Is she crazy? Why are you playing this game with her? Do you know what you're doing?*

"That's very kind of you," Carlotta stayed where she was, and looked very surprised when Manuela took her arm, as though they were friends. "Thank you, but it's not necessary. I don't need any help."

That was the moment when bells started to go off in Manuela's mind. She realized that Carlotta wasn't kidding.

"I'm going to look on my computer to see if I can find Mrs. Martin's address for you," Manuela promised, and led Carlotta into the kitchen.

"Have a seat while you're waiting. My daughter will keep you company and make you a cup of coffee."

"This is so kind of you," nodded Carlotta with a smile. She sat on one of the kitchen chairs.

"Carla, don't let her out of your sight, whatever you do," Manuela whispered to her daughter. "I don't think she knows who she is at the moment, or where she belongs. I'll be right back." Manuela left the kitchen and went directly to her office, where she shut the door behind her and reached for the telephone to call Mercy Ranch.

***

Cheryl and Ricki were on horseback. Sean had instructed them to ride along the same path that Carlotta had taken when she had fallen off Sheila.

"This is really far from the ranch," commented Cheryl. "She would never go this far on foot, especially since it's hard for her to walk. What do you think?"

Ricki bit her lip. "How do I know what a person does when they no longer know what they're doing? Wow, that was some sentence ... But honestly, I just can't imagine Carlotta losing it,

63

although she seemed a little strange after the fall, when I found her. But not knowing what's going on? I just can't wrap my brain around that. After all, your mind can't turn completely upside down from one day to the next!"

"Maybe Sean exaggerated a little," suggested Cheryl.

"Hmmm," Ricki considered that explanation for a moment. "But it doesn't make any sense to exaggerate. Why would he do that?"

"Maybe we should concentrate on just looking for her and not think about it so much. Maybe everything will clear up all by itself. I mean, after all, Carlotta can decide for herself where she goes and when, without telling anyone."

"That's true. And sometimes we can have really weird ideas and do things we would never normally do."

"Absolutely. For example, we could dismount and lead our horses straight through the woods so we'll reach Carlotta's riding path directly."

Ricki nodded.

"Yeah, let's do that. If we run through the woods, we'll get there faster than if we ride all the way around it. But we'd better not get caught by a forest ranger, or we'll get into trouble."

"Oh, no we won't." Cheryl just shoved aside the objection. "After all, it's an emergency. We're searching for a missing person."

"I bet no one would believe us. It seems so unlikely for someone to disappear around here."

"Whatever!" Cheryl jumped down from Sheila's saddle, and Ricki dismounted from Diablo. The two teenagers led their horses between the trees and through the dense woods.

"You can think whatever you want," Ricki said when

64

they finally reached the path, "but my gut tells me that we're on the wrong track."

"Why couldn't you have told me that a little sooner, before my arms got completely scratched up from all the low branches?"

"It wouldn't have helped you anyway. Sean told us to search this whole area." Ricki remounted and waited for Cheryl to get back in the saddle. She felt in her pocket for her cell phone. "I wish my phone would ring, and Kevin's mother would give us the all-clear signal."

"That would be great." Cheryl nodded, with a hint of a smile.

Silently, the two continued riding until the path met the road. At that point, they halted their horses, and wearily Cheryl suggested they turn back.

"If Carlotta's really on foot then she can't have gotten any farther than we did. With her bad leg, she'd probably have stopped long before this."

Ricki stared at a car that slowly drove past the two riders.

"Hey, are you even listening to me, Ricki? ... Ricki?"

Diablo's rider turned slowly toward Cheryl. "I think I'm hallucinating!"

"Why? Did you know that guy who was driving?"

"I think ... YES!"

"And?"

"And unless I'm mistaken, that was Diablo's former owner!"

Cheryl's mouth dropped open. "The guy who beat him and hit you with the bit? I thought he was in prison."

Ricki touched her collarbone that had been broken by the bit.

"That's the one. And the way it looks, he must be out! ...

65

Oh, no, you should have seen the way he looked at me! I'm positive he recognized me."

"And if not you, then for sure he recognized Diablo!"

"Gee, thanks, Cheryl. What a way to cheer me up." Ricki stroked her black horse with a shaky hand. "I won't have one peaceful minute knowing that he's out here again. I'm sure he hates me more than anything. After all, I was the reason he went to prison."

"Do you think he's going to try to get revenge?"

Ricki turned pale.

"I didn't want to say that so directly. But, you know, Cooper is the kind of guy who would hold a grudge forever, and he's real mean. It would be totally like him – Oh, no. I just hope he doesn't do anything to Diablo!"

"Or to you," added Cheryl apprehensively.

Ricki exhaled with a huge sigh. "Why are there so many problems in life just when you think everything's going well and you're happy?"

Cheryl shrugged her shoulders. "I have no idea, but, I'm sure he wouldn't dare come close to you. Do you honestly think he'd risk going back to jail again by hurting either you or Diablo?" she asked, trying to lift her friend's spirits.

"I hope not." Ricki let Diablo's reins loose and put her arms around herself for a moment's comfort. In spite of the summer heat, she felt a chill, and just thinking about Frank Cooper made her ill.

"I'm really scared, Cheryl," she said softly. "Not for me, but for Diablo. And I have no idea what I would do if that guy was suddenly standing in front of me."

***

After trying several times to reach someone at Mercy Ranch, Manuela finally gave up. She had tried just as

66

Caroline and Sean were outside, in front of the house, discussing how best to continue their search for Carlotta.

Darn it, she thought. Then she tried to think of what to do next. First of all, she had to go back to the kitchen and relieve Carla of watching over Carlotta.

As she reached the kitchen, she breathed a sigh of relief when she heard her daughter laughing. She looked at her questioningly.

Carla seemed to be saying, "Everything's okay" with her look.

Carlotta looked up, too.

"Manuela! It's great to find you here. I want to talk to you about the event tomorrow," she said, completely normal, as though nothing had happened. "When are you arriving with Sid? The ranch opens for visitors at nine a.m., and I think most of the people will come between ten and three."

"Hello, Carlotta." Somewhat unsure of the situation, she greeted her friend again. "I didn't think I'd see you again today. You could have saved yourself the trip. That's why we have telephones."

"I wouldn't have gotten any coffee on the phone," grinned Carlotta. She seemed to be her old self again.

After Manuela poured herself a cup of coffee, the two women talked about the open house, and for the next hour and a half the photographer forgot about her friend's strange behavior.

"Okay, then let's leave it like that: you two will come about noon," said Carlotta, getting up and glancing at her watch. "Oh, it's so late already. I didn't notice how quickly the time has gone. I'd better be getting home."

Manuela nodded in agreement and then the two women went outside.

Carlotta looked around, searching for something.

"Where's my car? I parked it here in front."

Manuela bit her lip and then she took her friend's arm and walked her back into the house and into the kitchen.

"Carlotta, we need to have a talk," she said gently, if a little awkwardly, as the older woman seated herself at the table.

"How are you?" Manuela asked.

"I'm fine, if you don't count the fact that my car has disappeared."

"You're sure you're all right?"

Carlotta was starting to get uncomfortable with the line of questioning.

"What do you mean? Why do you keep asking me how I am? It would be better if you told me where my car is," she answered, sounding upset. Manuela put her hand on Carlotta's, trying to calm her down.

"Don't get upset."

"I am upset. It isn't possible that –"

"Carlotta, your car is probably at the ranch."

"What? That's nonsense. I drove here."

Manuela shook her head slowly.

"I didn't? But how did –?"

"You were on foot."

Carlotta looked at her friend and laughed.

"Manuela, are you crazy? Why would I come all this way on foot? I can't waste my valuable time going for a walk when I have so much to do. And with this thing." She raised the crutch that she had never been without since her riding accident many years ago. "What nonsense!"

But when she saw Manuela's serious expression, she cleared her throat and said nothing.

After a moment of silence Manuela tried again.

"When did you leave Mercy Ranch? What time was it?"

"I have no idea. I didn't look at my watch," answered Carlotta brusquely and put her hand to her forehead.

"Do you have a headache?"

"Yes. The whole day. Maybe the weather is changing."

"I think you should go see your doctor. You have headaches far too often."

Carlotta's glance wandered to the window and then lost itself on the paddock in front of the house.

"You say I didn't drive here?" she asked, suddenly eerily calm.

"That's right."

"Hmmm ... then it must be true. I –" she turned to her friend. "In the last few weeks I've been very forgetful, and I can't seem to keep track of time and ... Manuela, I was at the doctor."

"Oh. And what did he say?" The photographer sensed that it was difficult for her friend to go on.

Carlotta, who was never at a loss for words, was now obviously very upset, and Manuela had to concentrate hard in order to understand what she was saying, practically in a whisper.

"I have a tumor in my head. It's pressing on the area of my brain that controls short-term memory. That's why I keep forgetting things, and why I can't remember some things at all. It's also affecting my sight, which is why I've had such problems with my eyes lately."

"A tumor?" Manuela was shocked. She had thought of many possibilities, but not something like that.

"I've known for quite some time. Actually, I was supposed to have had an operation three weeks ago." She laughed uneasily. "But would you let someone operate on you without knowing how you'll be afterward? I still have so much to do, but if it doesn't go well, then there's a chance that I won't be able to do anything. Do you understand what I mean? What would happen to the ranch then?"

She swallowed hard, and when she saw Manuela's pale, frightened face, it was she who patted Manuela's hand. "Mercy Ranch and the horses ... so much depends on me. I can't –"

"You're afraid." said Manuela all of a sudden. "It's not the work that's keeping you from having this operation. It's fear, isn't it? But you're not helping anyone if the tumor keeps getting bigger. You keep saying that it's the ranch and the horses, but what will happen if you don't have the operation? Sure, with an operation there's always a risk, but I'm sure that the chance of you getting well is greater than the chance of you losing everything, right? And I think it's more likely that you'll lose, if you don't have the operation. Carlotta, I'm begging you, go to the hospital, have the operation. In a few weeks, everything will be okay."

Carlotta was silent for a few seconds. For now, she was not willing to agree to Manuela's urgent plea. The conversation she'd had with her doctor was still very much on her mind, and what he said was anything but encouraging. However, if she couldn't even remember whether or not she had driven to Manuela's, then she really did have to deal with the operation while she was still in control of her senses.

As Carlotta got up wearily, Manuela felt as though her friend had aged several years in the last ten minutes.

"Can you drive me home?"

"Of course."

"It was good to talk about it, finally. Thank you," Carlotta said softly. "It will all happen the way it's supposed to happen. Don't be sad." Then she slowly walked to the door while Manuela fought back her tears.

Chapter 5

Caroline Thomas sighed with relief when she looked out the window and saw Manuela drive up with Carlotta. Before she went outside she dialed Sean's cell phone to call off the search.

"She's back," she said, her voice trembling. "You can tell the kids to come home." Without waiting for Sean's answer, she hung up and ran outside.

"Where in the world were you? You've been gone so long and we were worried sick."

Carlotta got out of the car and looked at Caroline ruefully.

"Manuela will explain it to you," she said briefly, and then she limped slowly toward the house. It was obvious that walking was difficult. The distance she had gone on foot had been too much for her.

Caroline wanted to hurry after her, but Manuela shook her head no.

"Let her go. I think she'd like to be alone right now," she said softly.

"But I can't –"

"Please let her go." Manuela looked at her intensely.

"What's wrong with her?"

The photographer was silent for a moment, and then she put her arm around Kevin's mother.

"I'll tell you everything. Let's go in the kitchen."

"Of course," answered Caroline, hoarsely. Her concern for Carlotta was deep, and Manuela's look only confirmed that her worry was justified.

Silently, she walked back into the house with Manuela, wondering what news she was about to hear.

***

"Whew, I am so glad she's back," said Ricki, relieved, after Sean's call. Even her thoughts of Diablo's former owner slipped away in her joy that Carlotta had turned up.

"Imagine what would happen if any of us just disappeared like that," laughed Cheryl. "Carlotta would really make a scene."

"She would be merciless with us," suggested Ricki.

"You can be sure of it. That's one advantage of being grown up. You can do almost anything you want without having to answer for it," responded Cheryl.

"But to go somewhere without telling anyone is just plain dumb, don't you think? She could at least have told Sean that she was going to be gone for a while."

Cheryl shrugged her shoulders.

"Carlotta is old enough to know what she's doing."

"But she caused all of us so much worry that could have been avoided by just saying something before she left."

"Ricki, let her enjoy her little excursion. She has so

much on her plate, maybe she needed to get away for a while. And anyway, you have to look at it positively. We got to go for a really nice ride, didn't we?"

"Hmmm, it would have been nicer if – Oh, whatever. She's back and that's the important thing."

"Exactly. And I'm sure she's really happy that the tents are up and the horses are groomed, and that –"

"And that it won't be our fault if tomorrow isn't a huge success." Ricki finished her friend's thought.

"That's what I was going to say. Hey, how about a little gallop before we go back?"

"A gallop would be great." Ricki shortened the reins and beamed at Cheryl. "A race to the bend in the path?"

"You'll lose anyway," laughed Cheryl as Sheila galloped off.

"Just you wait. You don't stand a chance!" Ricki called after her, and then Diablo galloped off. After only a few yards he passed Sheila, the Black Forest mare, with long strides.

"Bye," Ricki leaned flat over her horse's neck and whispered to him, "Show 'em what you can do, my sweetie. Sheila will turn green with envy!" Then she laughed lightly and enjoyed the sensation of her horse's strength. All of the thoughts that had burdened Ricki in the last two hours were gone.

He's like dynamite! The thought occurred to her as she felt her black horse go faster and faster. *Like dynamite but still as gentle as a lamb!* Never before had she known a horse so full of contradictions.

Diablo was a fast, courageous tower of strength, and Ricki could always rely on him one hundred percent. He would give his all, if necessary, and he would go through fire – or worse – for Ricki. On the other hand, he was the most affectionate, gentle horse the girl had ever known. Loving and sometimes playful like a colt, other times challenging and stubborn, he always tried to do what his rider and her friends wanted of him.

He is one unique horse, thought Ricki, happily, overjoyed that he belonged to her.

What could be more wonderful than a life with Diablo?

As Ricki rode through the lush, green summer landscape, she forgot everything around her. The regular beat of his hooves seemed to move in rhythm with the beating of her heart, and, in moments like these, she felt at one with her horse more than at any other time.

"Okay, I give up," she heard Cheryl's voice call from far behind her. "Ricki! Ricki!"

Breathless, Ricki sat up in the saddle and slowly brought Diablo to a stop. What a shame. The gallop ended much too soon, and she almost regretted that she wasn't alone. She could have gone on galloping forever.

But now she needed a few seconds to get back to reality. She turned her horse around and started toward a grinning Cheryl.

"Well, today you must have filled up with the wrong gas," she teased merrily, as Sheila finally caught up.

"We thought we'd let you win for once," Cheryl claimed.

"Yeah, yeah, of course."

Then the two of them broke out laughing.

Together they rode the last few yards to Mercy Ranch, where they unsaddled their horses and sprayed them with water to cool them off, and then turned them out on the paddock to join their friends for the rest of the evening.

Walking over to the stable, they noticed that the ranch was particularly quiet. Where was everyone?

When the girls entered the stable, they saw their friends in the corridor, sitting opposite one another on bales of hay, their faces grim, talking quietly. They hadn't noticed the pair of staring eyes observing them the entire time.

***

"So this is where you brought him," mumbled the man excitedly, and if anyone had seen him, they would have noticed that he was full of hate. "You nasty little stable rat. You and that darned horse stole two years of my life! I'll make you sorry for that! I swear it! You can't do that to Frank Cooper without repercussions!"

His eyes gleamed furiously as he worked on a horrible plan.

For a few more minutes, he looked over Mercy Ranch through binoculars; then his glance focused on a large blackboard that was set up at the ranch's entrance.

Sunday, June 21
Open House
Experience an Unforgettable
Day at Mercy Ranch

With a mean grin, he showed his teeth. "That's good," he mumbled softly to himself. "That's *very good*!"

Disgusted, he spat, and then turned and disappeared behind the dense bushes that lined the driveway, back toward his car. There was a lot to prepare before he could take his revenge tomorrow.

"It will definitely be an unforgettable day. I can guarantee you that, Ricki Sulai."

"I think we should call the whole thing off for tomorrow," Kieran was saying as Cheryl and Ricki approached the kids. "There's just no sense in it if Carlotta isn't well. What do you guys think?"

The girls listened in stunned silence.

"You heard what Sean said," countered Hal. "She doesn't want the open house to be cancelled on her account."

"But it won't be the same if she's not there."

"You can say that again," sighed Kevin. "Does anyone know exactly what's wrong with her? Sean won't say anything if you ask him. That's suspicious."

"I think we have a right to know what's wrong with Carlotta," Ricki called out sharply, as she and Cheryl made their way down the corridor to where their friends were gathered.

"Oh, really? How do you figure that? I think if that were the case, someone would have already told us." Hal stretched his back. "But I sure would like to know."

"Well, maybe my mom will tell us something tonight." Kevin said hopefully.

"Anyway, I don't have a good feeling as far as Carlotta is concerned," said Ricki.

"You and your feelings," her boyfriend teased.

"I can't help it if I can usually sense when something is going on, can I?" Ricki defended herself.

The two looked at each other, and, after a moment of silence, Kieran stood up.

"I think we should stop for today. Everything is ready for tomorrow. Sean said that he wants to leave the horses on the paddock for at least two more hours and then he's going to bring them into their stalls himself. So I think I'll go home now. It's going to be a long day tomorrow and I'm really beat."

Hal nodded. "I'll say goodbye, too. Cheryl, are you coming?"

"Yeah. I bet I'll sleep like a baby tonight," she said, yawning.

"Well then, see you guys tomorrow morning – early!" the kids said to Ricki and Kevin as they left the stable. "Take good care of our boss. Don't let her take off again," said Hal, before getting on his bike.

"Stupid joke," whispered Ricki and then waved to them. She turned to Kevin.

"I think I'm going to take a shower, if that's okay."

"Of course!"

"Great! ... You know, I'm really glad I don't have to go home tonight. It was nice of your mom to let me to stay here overnight."

"Yeah, I'm glad, too," Kevin grinned.

"The only problem is you'd better not snore so loud that I can hear you in the next room," she said and winked at him.

"And what if I do?"

"Then I'll sleep outside with Diablo."

Kevin groaned, exaggerating it a bit too much.

"Diablo will always be my rival, won't he?" he asked.

But Ricki shook her head. "There is no competition. Even you can't manage to compete with him."

"Well, that's encouraging. All right, come on, you horse fanatic. I'll grab you a towel, and then you can take your beauty bath."

Smiling, he put his arm around his girlfriend and together they slowly walked to the house.

Carlotta, who had watched the two of them from her office window, stepped back and collapsed onto her chair.

It would be wonderful to be young again, she thought. *Free of worries, healthy ...* She sighed and stared at the telephone, and then she picked up the receiver and dialed. But when someone answered at the other end of the line, she couldn't remember what she had wanted to say. When she realized it, she covered her face with her hands.

For the first time in many, many years, she cried.

***

It had been dark for some time when a vehicle with a horse trailer approached Mercy Ranch without its headlights on. When it reached the first paddock, the driver turned onto a side road and turned the motor off. For a moment the flame from a lighter was visible, and then the glow of a cigarette.

Frank Cooper was nervous, but determined to do what he had planned.

He gazed steadily at the dark ranch.

It wouldn't be easy to get Diablo out of there, especially since there were two dogs that could start to bark, but he would manage somehow.

Determined, he got out of the car and was just about to lower the loading ramp of the trailer when he noticed that almost all of the lights in the house suddenly went on.

Swearing softly, he hid behind the bushes and kept the ranch in sight.

"What's that about?" he grumbled quietly to himself. It looked like he would have to abandon his plan.

***

"Have I already told you ..." began Ricki for the third time in ten minutes, and Kevin groaned.

They were in Kevin's room, where Ricki was excitedly going over the plans for tomorrow.

"C'mon, Ricki, not again. Can't you please stop? I thought you were so tired. When are you going to sleep?" The boy yawned loudly. "I can't keep my eyes open anymore. Every time I'm about to fall asleep, you start yakking again."

"Yeah, sorry, but now I'm too tired to sleep. Too worked up, or something. But have I already told you that Mrs. Highland is coming tomorrow with Gwendolyn, and Gwen said –"

"Who cares if she's coming to visit her friend Carlotta and bringing her granddaughter with her? Now, go to sleep," Kevin grumbled and pulled the blanket over his head.

Ricki sighed and left for the guestroom.

Sleep? Not a chance. She was much too excited to go to sleep. Not only was tomorrow the open house, but her friend Gwendolyn was coming, which was fantastic. She had been to Highland Farms Estate for several vacations with her friends and their horses, and she had had several adventures with Gwen, but tomorrow was the first time that Gwen would be coming here. She was bringing her horse, Black Jack, and she and her grandmother were going to stay at the ranch for several days.

How cool is that, thought Ricki. They could go riding together, and she was sure that Gwen would find the area around Echo Lake as beautiful as she. Gwen would also finally get to meet Jake and Oliver, whom Ricki had told her all about.

Ricki turned her face to the window and stared at the crescent moon, which was covered by a veil of fog.

So Gwen would be here, and Lillian, too, which thrilled Ricki almost as much. If Cathy could be here, too, then the gang would be complete. But no, she'd fallen down the stupid stairs. Her accident couldn't have come at a worse time!

The major thing that upset Ricki was that Carlotta wasn't well. She was sure that it was only temporary, and when the stress of the open house was over Carlotta would be able to take it easy for a while. At least she would feel better having her old friend Eleanor Highland come for a visit. Ricki was certain about that.

The girl closed her eyes.

Maybe I should try to sleep a little, she thought. *If I don't, I'll be completely useless tomorrow!*

For quite a while she lay there motionless, but all of a sudden she sat straight up and listened in the darkness.

What was that sound she heard? Could it be mice? She bolted from the bed and rushed next door to Kevin's room.

"Kevin? Kevin! Are there mice in the house?" she asked loudly.

"Arrrghhh! I can't believe it. Here you go again. Ricki, I swear, if you don't stop talking, this is the last time you get to sleep over."

"Yeah, but are there mice or not?"

Kevin sat up in bed, in a bad mood. His eyes were glaring moodily.

"No. There are no mice here. Are you satisfied now?"

Ricki didn't answer. She kept listening.

"Hey, can't you hear that? What is it?"

"That's what happens when you stay awake and don't sleep. You start imagining things."

Ricki pulled off Kevin's blanket. "Don't be ridiculous. I'm not crazy. You have to hear something. It's getting louder!"

"I don't hear a thing. There's nothing here," Kevin groaned. "If it'll make you feel better I'll go and look, but that's the last thing I'm going to do tonight. If you still don't – Now what's wrong?"

This time it wasn't a little mouse-like sound that the two teens heard. It was the sound of a vehicle driving fast toward the house, with a rotating blue light on top that lit up Kevin's room eerily.

Ricki rushed to the window and stared with horror at the ambulance suddenly parked out front.

Not two seconds later, Kevin stood behind her. Frightened, they looked at each other.

"Carlotta!"

Then both of them ran out of the room.

Chapter 6

Carlotta lay on the floor of the bathroom. Caroline knelt next to her and held her hand while Sean opened the door for the two EMS technicians and the emergency doctor.

"Get out of the way!" he yelled at Ricki and Kevin, who were standing pale as ghosts in front of the bathroom door, staring at Carlotta.

Ricki almost stumbled as she stepped aside for the EMS workers and bumped into Kevin. Everything was happening so quickly.

The men took Carlotta out to the ambulance on a gurney. Caroline got in, and then, with sirens blaring, off they went to the hospital.

Sean explained to the kids, in brusque fragments, what had happened, and then he jumped in his car to drive to the hospital.

"She fell ... was unconscious ... didn't wake up. Take care of the ranch until I'm back."

Sean's words burned into Ricki and Kevin's brains, and now that everything in the house was once again silent, Ricki's legs began to give way. Silently, tears of fear for Carlotta flowed down her cheeks as her knees buckled and she landed on the floor.

Kevin, fear showing on his face, sat down next to her and put his arm around her.

"It's ... I'm sure it's not as bad as it looks," he tried to comfort Ricki, but she shook her head forlornly and looked at the floor.

"I think, that ... that ... it's even worse than we think. And you know what's even worse than that, Kevin? Sitting here and having no idea what's wrong with Carlotta and what's going on at the hospital right now."

"Mom will tell us. I'm sure of that."

Ricki cuddled up in her boyfriend's arms and was glad that she could lean on him.

"Couldn't we just get our bikes and ride to the hospital?" she asked, as she sniffed back her tears. But Kevin reminded her of what Sean had said.

"We're supposed to take care of the ranch. I'm sure Carlotta wouldn't want us to leave the horses alone. After all, you never know ..."

Ricki looked at him with wide eyes.

"What do you mean by that? 'You never know'."

Kevin cleared his throat. "Well, there were a few suspicious phone calls recently, so it's just better if we keep our eyes open here."

Naturally, Ricki would have liked to ask what kind of calls they were, but she didn't. She sensed that she couldn't handle any more tension than she already felt.

"Kevin ... I'm glad you're here," she whispered instead,

and wished that the night was over and Sean or Caroline were back home so she could get some answers about Carlotta's condition.

***

Frank Cooper watched Carlotta being taken away by ambulance. He also noticed that two adults had gone with her, but since he didn't know how many adults were at the ranch, and since there were lights on everywhere in the house and in the yard, he decided to postpone his plans for the night.

Ten minutes after the ambulance left, and he was sure that the car following the ambulance wouldn't be back, he started his car and left his hiding place. He drove to the main road, where he finally turned on his headlights and drove off quickly, unseen by anyone.

He would find another way to get to the horse – the horse *and* the girl.

***

Ricki didn't know how long she had been sitting on the floor with Kevin until she heard the door shut and the dogs barking their greeting.

"It's okay." she heard Sean's tired voice.

"Kevin. Kevin, wake up. Sean's back." Gently, Ricki shook her boyfriend awake. He had fallen asleep sitting there. She looked at her watch. Four hours had gone by since Carlotta had been picked up. Four long hours that had seemed like an eternity to the girl.

Kevin rubbed his eyes, suddenly wide awake.

Together they got up, holding hands like little children, and walked down the hallway.

Sean looked at the two of them for a long time without saying anything.

Ricki began to tremble.

"What ... what's happening with Carlotta? Is she ... is she ...?" She couldn't say the word.

Sean took a deep breath and then he shook his head.

"They're performing emergency surgery on her. There's a tumor pressing on the main artery to her brain."

"What? A tumor?" The kids were paralyzed by fear.

Sean nodded. "They had to call in a specialist, which wasn't easy in the middle of the night. But they're operating now and we can only hope and pray that she'll survive. Kevin, your mother decided to stay at the hospital."

Sean put his hands on Kevin's shoulders.

"Carlotta ... she just can't die," whispered Ricki, almost unable to speak. She looked pleadingly at Sean. But as much as he would have liked to tell her something encouraging, he couldn't, because Carlotta's life seemed to be hanging by a silk thread.

Kevin stared into the distance.

"What about tomorrow? Should we put out a sign that the open house is canceled? I don't think any of us will feel like doing it now."

Sean's weariness seemed to recede as he straightened up defiantly and put his hands on his waist.

"No. We're going to have this event, and we're going to do it just as Carlotta wanted." He tried to smile. "You know her, she'd be furious if we didn't go through with it because of her. And of course, that's the first thing she's going to ask as soon as she can talk."

Kevin and Ricki lowered their heads. They sensed that even Sean didn't believe what he was saying.

"Go to bed now and try to get some sleep. There's

nothing else you can do. You two have a busy day tomorrow. We owe it to Carlotta to make sure that this open house is a huge success." Sean nudged the two of them toward the stairs leading to the bedrooms.

"It's impossible to sleep now," responded Ricki. Although she was exhausted, she knew that she would lie awake for the rest of the night, and that Kevin would, too. Nevertheless, they did what Sean wanted, especially since they sensed that Kevin's future stepfather was struggling with his feelings as much as they were. He, too, couldn't imagine what it would mean to lose Carlotta, and he needed time to deal with the situation. At the same time, his thoughts were with Caroline, and he asked himself if he did the right thing by leaving her at the hospital, all alone.

***

Ricki and Kevin both had fallen into a leaden, weary sleep toward morning, and awoke completely exhausted when they heard someone call from the downstairs hallway. "Are you two awake yet?" It was Sean.

"Oh, no," groaned Ricki, still half asleep, but a few seconds later, when she realized what had happened during the night, she jumped up and ran next door to Kevin's room.

"Kevin. Kevin. Did you hear your mother come home last night?" Impatiently, she shook her boyfriend.

"Nope, I didn't hear anything." Then he looked at his alarm clock." Seven o'clock ... Oh, no, tell me that last night was just something I dreamed."

"I wish." Ricki was about to leave to get changed when there was a knock on the door, and she pulled it open.

"Good, you're up. I've got breakfast ready. Want some?" Sean asked from the doorway. He also looked as if he had barely slept.

"Definitely. We'll be down in a minute." replied Kevin and forced himself to get up.

Not five minutes later, they were downstairs in the kitchen with Sean.

"Is there any news?"

Sean shrugged his shoulders.

"Your mother called. Carlotta survived the surgery but she was put into an induced coma to keep her still. The doctors plan to wake her up in about forty eight hours. At the moment it doesn't look very good."

"Oh, no." Ricki collapsed onto a kitchen chair.

Sean bit his lip, and then he straightened his shoulders and tried a smile.

"We won't help Carlotta by being so gloomy. We have to believe that she'll make it. And until she's back with us, we're all going to do everything possible to keep the ranch going as usual."

Kevin nodded, but Ricki could tell that a thousand thoughts were running through his mind.

"I know that this isn't being positive," he began slowly, "but what if she doesn't make it?"

"Kevin! You mustn't say that!" Ricki burst out.

"I know, but what would happen to the ranch and to the horses?"

Sean stood with his back to the kids and poured glasses of juice. Slowly he turned around, put the glasses on the table, and looked at them seriously.

"Carlotta had a short period of clarity yesterday, before she was rolled into the operating room. She told your mother that we, Caroline and I, should take over the ranch if anything happens to her, so that everything can go on as it is. And that we should always remember that the horses come first, and that we should do everything possible to make sure that the animals are well taken care of." Tears filled his eyes and he brushed them away with the back of his hand.

"She ... she had a nurse write it all down and then she signed it in front of witnesses."

Kevin took a deep breath. "That means she signed the ranch over to you both?"

Sean nodded.

"With all the rights and duties of ownership, if we're willing to take over Mercy Ranch and continue it," he explained.

"And? Are you willing?" asked Ricki hesitantly.

Sean's gaze wandered into the distance.

"Yes, although we know that would also mean a good-bye."

"I understand ..." Kevin took Ricki's hand. "As soon as we have our breakfast, we're going to feed the horses and brush them. The others will be here soon. You probably have lots of things to do."

Sean nodded gratefully. "Yes. And we can't forget that people will start coming in about two hours."

"How could we forget that?"

As Sean left to tend to last-minute details, Ricki couldn't hold back her sobs any longer.

"I just can't believe it. It can't be true!" she cried. "Carlotta is giving up the ranch ... She ... she would never do that if she had any hope, would she, Kevin?"

"Please, Ricki, I don't know. Maybe we should just try to make the day go well."

"How can I make the day go well, when I don't know if she's going to survive it? How can you be so insensitive, Kevin?"

"I'm *not* insensitive, but we promised Carlotta that we would do our best and that's what I'm going to do – even if she doesn't know what's going on here. I just want to keep my promise. Can you understand that, Ricki? If I don't start working I'm going to go crazy." Kevin's voice was hard. He got up, left the kitchen, and forcefully walked toward the stable. Ricki followed behind, looking at him sadly.

"Carlotta wouldn't want us to fight," she commented softly as Kevin lifted the feed buckets.

"Then let's get to work. She'd be furious with us if she knew that the horses still haven't been fed."

***

It was barely half an hour later when Kieran, Hal, and Cheryl arrived in fairly good moods. Their smiles faded pretty quickly, however, when they found out what had happened overnight. Even Lillian, who came a few minutes later, had few words.

"Is she okay? Is she allowed to have visitors?" she asked.

"Probably not yet," replied Kevin. But no one had any real answers.

The kids got to work, their spirits very much dampened. Kieran and Hal dragged crates of beverages into one of the tents and set up the grill on one of the tables, where the hot dogs were going to be cooked for the visitors. Cheryl put out the plates, which had been loaned by a local caterer, and Lillian filled in for Caroline by preparing the salads that were going to be served.

Ricki and Kevin took the horses out to the paddock after their breakfasts. Afterward, they helped Sean quickly clean the stalls. Finally it was 9:00, and the doors of Mercy

Ranch were opened wide for the guests who, hopefully, would be arriving in large groups any minute.

"I'm already exhausted," groaned Cheryl, and she leaned against Hal.

"There is one benefit to keeping busy," he said. "At least we don't have any time to think about anything."

***

At 9:30 the first guests arrived at the ranch. They walked through the stable and looked in all the stalls with interest, and then toured the grounds. While the adult guests learned about the mission of the ranch, their children played in the paddock area and stroked the horses, which came to the fence, curious about all the people who had come. The horses enjoyed all the attention.

One woman was particularly interested in Diablo, and Ricki worked hard trying to convince her that he was not one of the horses who belonged at the ranch and was therefore not for sale.

"I think it was a mistake to have Sharazan and Diablo here today," she groaned. "It looks like they're stealing the show from the other animals. The people are supposed to be interested in the ranch's horses."

"Maybe it would be better to bring them to the little paddock behind the house," suggested Kieran.

"That's a great idea. I'll take them over there right away." Ricki nodded and ran off.

By noon the ranch had filled up, and Lillian and Cheryl had their hands full feeding all the guests.

"Tonight I'm going to dream about grilled hot dogs and potato salad," said Cheryl with a grin. Lillian said she couldn't bear the sight of one more cupcake.

Hal had separated off a little bit of meadow on the

91

paddock, where he entertained the youngest guests with a game of horseshoes and a horse drawing competition. The children were thrilled because they all won something they could take home with them.

Kevin and Ricki ran back and forth to help out wherever they were needed. At two o'clock they planned to saddle Sharazan and Diablo so they could give the children rides for an hour. About a half hour before that, Josh and his Western friends would arrive at the ranch and give their performance.

Outwardly, all of them seemed to be in a good mood, although inside they felt very different. There was no one who didn't think about Carlotta the whole time, and they were very glad to be distracted from the tragedy by all the activities.

Just before noon, Manuela, Carla, and Sid arrived, as did Mrs. Charles Osgood Highland III, horse breeder and owner of Highland Farms Estate and her granddaughter, Gwendolyn. Gwen had brought her horse, Black Jack, in a horse trailer.

Sean saw them arrive and signaled to Kieran to take over the conversation he was having with some of the visitors who were standing around him. Then he went over to greet the new arrivals.

"You must be the legendary Sean, of whom Carlotta has spoken so highly." Eleanor Highland reached out her hand happily.

Sean shook her hand, slightly embarrassed by the praise.

"She told me she was very lucky to find you."

"Well ..."

"Where is my friend anyway? If I know her – and I have for ages – she's probably around somewhere trying to turn every single guest into a crusader against animal cruelty." Mrs. Highland looked all around the grounds, trying to catch sight of her old friend.

Gwendolyn, meanwhile, had discovered Ricki and quickly ran over to her.

"Ricki, I'm so happy to see you!" she called out and threw her arms around her friend. Then she caught sight of Lillian over Ricki's shoulder, standing at a sales booth in one of the tents. "Whoa, I can't believe it. Lillian is well again. Hey, Lillian. Lily!" And she was off to greet the girl as warmly as she had greeted Ricki.

"I'm so glad you're okay. How's your leg? Is it back to normal? And anyway – Oh, it's so wonderful to see you all again."

"Gwendolyn! Come here and take Black Jack out of the trailer," her grandmother called out loudly.

"Yes, Granny, right away," replied Gwen. "Ricki, where can I put Black Jack?"

"You can bring him to the paddock with Diablo and Sharazan. Come with me, I'll show you where it is." Ricki's eyes beamed with pleasure, and for a moment she actually forgot about Carlotta.

"Okay, and then you have to tell me all the news here."

Uh-oh. Suddenly Ricki's expression changed and everything that had happened last night came to the forefront, as though it had just happened minutes ago.

"Carlotta had to have an emergency operation last night ... a brain tumor," she explained sadly as she walked beside her friend to the trailer.

"What? Say that again!" Gwen stood stock-still and stared at Ricki in disbelief. Instead of repeating what she had said, Ricki just nodded with a sorrowful face.

"That's unbelievable. Granny! Granny!" Gwen ran over to her grandmother, but when she reached her and saw her pale face, she knew that she had just learned the sad news from Sean.

Manuela, who had also heard what Sean had said, stood next to the others, shocked, and listened to Sean as he did his best to fill them in on the details.

"For heaven's sakes, why didn't she tell me about her health problems?" Mrs. Highland thundered. "We call each other every two or three days and she couldn't even tell her best friend the truth." She paced back and forth, thoroughly upset. "Whenever I asked her how she was, she'd always say, 'Oh, I'm fine. Everything's fine.' ... Oh, what a good actress she was. I could just scream that I didn't notice anything. I can assure you, I would have taken her to the hospital myself, immediately."

"She wouldn't let anyone take her anywhere," said Manuela gravely.

"I know, but I would have done it anyway. Somehow," countered Mrs. Highland.

Sean glanced at the people standing nearby who were listening intently.

"Let's continue this inside. I don't think everyone has to hear this," he said softly, but Mrs. Highland snorted like a wild stallion.

"As far as I'm concerned, everyone can listen," she said, her voice raised in anger for all to hear. "Carlotta, the most loving, caring person in the whole world, is sick. She worked herself into exhaustion for the horses on Mercy Ranch twenty-four hours a day, seven days a week, to see that they had the best care. Every day she fought with people who mistreat horses and moved heaven and earth

94

to make a better life for the animals without ever thinking of herself. Why can't people here see that one person alone can't solve the problems of abused animals without harming herself? They have to see the connection. What use is it for them to come to this open house and see how good the ranch and the animals look, eat a lot, have a good time, and then go home without supporting that person in any way – that wonderful, selfless woman who has given her all in order to create all this and more?" Mrs. Highland had become very agitated.

Manuela raised her camera automatically and took Mrs. Highland's picture, while Sid recorded her speech.

"Granny, please ..." Gwen tried to calm her down, but Eleanor just whirled around and yelled at her.

"What's true is true." She said, and her granddaughter was immediately silenced.

She turned to the guests at Mercy Ranch, who were now standing in groups around her. "It's useless just to make nice speeches. This ranch needs practical help and support in order to achieve its goals. I bet there are some people here that may consider adopting or fostering a horse after this visit, but considering isn't enough. For many, by next week Mercy Ranch will be forgotten and everything will be back to the way it was."

She took a deep breath and continued, her eyes penetrating the crowds. "My best friend, the owner of this ranch, is lying in a coma after a serious operation, and no one knows if she will ever wake up. Her last thought, however, before she was wheeled into the operating room, was that the ranch had to continue and that there have to be people willing to fight to save abused animals and to help see that the abusers are not permitted to get away with their crimes. That was the reason for this event and why she didn't want it called off because of her. Now, if you people came here just to show your children what a horse looks like, you are in the wrong place."

The visitors began to talk among themselves, and there were some who grabbed their children and stormed toward their cars.

"How insulting."

"Who does she think she is?"

"This is unbelievable. What gives her the right to talk to us like that?"

Sean was visibly distressed, but in spite of Eleanor's emotional speech, most of the people stayed and looked at each other with embarrassment.

"Gwendolyn, get Black Jack out of the trailer. Sean, would you be so kind as to unhook the trailer? I have to get to the hospital. I have to know how Carlotta is doing."

Sean nodded, and right after Gwen had unloaded her horse Mrs. Highland roared off with screeching tires and without uttering another word.

For a few seconds, there was absolute silence at the ranch, and then a voice from the crowd of guests asked, "Who was that?"

Sean turned to the speaker and answered, "That was Mrs. Charles Osgood Highland III, the owner of Highland Farms Estate, the internationally famous horse-breeding farm."

"Oh, but does that give her the right to talk to us like that? Is *she* involved with Mercy Ranch?"

"Most certainly. Without the financial backing of Mrs. Highland, Mercy Ranch would never have been able to exist. But considering how many horses are suffering, her help is only a drop in the ocean, and we need many more donations in order to secure the lodging and food for the animals we have and those to come."

Sean then faced the audience who had gathered around. "Ladies and gentlemen, I'm sorry if Mrs. Highland's words offended you, but I ask for your understanding. She had just found out that her oldest friend, Carlotta Mancini, owner of Mercy Ranch, is lying in the hospital, fighting for her life. Her nerves were raw, and I would like you –"

Just then a man stepped forward from the crowd and smiled at Sean.

"You don't have to apologize for the honest words of that lady. She was right. I always appreciate it when people say what they mean." He held out his hand to Sean.

"May I introduce myself? The name's Kimmel. Louis Kimmel."

"A pleasure. Sean Devlin."

The two men shook hands.

"Mr. Devlin, I think we should have a talk. I'm the owner of a large car dealership and I love horses. Let's think about how I could help you. By the way, that Mrs. Highland ... she's a wonderful woman. I liked her." He laughed and his white teeth flashed.

Another man joined them.

"Carter Webster, general contractor. I can see that your barn isn't in the best condition. I could offer to renovate the entire building. For free, of course. Would that be acceptable?"

Sean didn't know what to say.

Gradually, more and more people came up to him, and with each one, he set up an appointment to talk further. He never had thought that Mrs. Highland's words would have such a strong effect on the guests and cause such a wave of offers to help Mercy Ranch.

As he disappeared into Carlotta's office with the two men who'd spoken up first, the rest of the visitors wandered off to look over the grounds and the horses.

Ricki and her friends stood together almost paralyzed, staring in the direction Eleanor Highland had disappeared.

"Your grandmother is just like Carlotta," announced Kieran, with admiration. "She says what she thinks."

Gwen sighed. "Oh, yeah, but today she was in especially good form. The news about Carlotta is really awful."

Lillian nodded absently. "I didn't know that it was *so* serious," she said softly.

"None of us did, exactly," answered Ricki, her voice cracking. As she spoke, she saw a horse transporter driving off down the road, and registered it unconsciously.

"I'd like to put Black Jack in the paddock now. Is that okay?" Gwen stroked her black horse's neck.

"Of course." Ricki took a deep breath and ran on ahead, as her friends went back to their stations. "Come on."

"What a speech," marveled Sid, and he turned off his recorder. "This is going to be a great story. Did you get the photos?"

"Sure did," Manuela answered, but her thoughts were elsewhere. "I hope Carlotta makes it," she said quietly. "She doesn't deserve to die like this."

Chapter 7

Ricki walked toward the paddock beside Gwen and Black Jack with her gaze lowered, and she told her friend what had happened during the night.

Sharazan came up to the gate just as Ricki was about to open it.

"Hey, move over," she said. "You've got a visitor." And while Gwen tried to get her horse onto the paddock without letting Sharazan escape, she asked Ricki, "Where's your beauty?"

"Back there."

"Where?"

Instantly Ricki's head flew up and her heart skipped a beat.

Diablo was nowhere to be seen.

"Could he have jumped the fence?"

"He's never done anything like that before, and he

wouldn't," Ricki said hoarsely, holding on to the poles of the fence to keep from collapsing.

Suddenly she pounded her fist into the wood.

"Why is it always Diablo? Oh no, what did I do that people think they have to take my horse away from me? It's unbelievable. He was here half an hour ago. Gwen, this is making me crazy." Ricki sobbed loudly, and in desperation kicked one of the poles at the entrance to the paddock, causing it to wobble. Suddenly a piece of paper, which had probably been stuck between two boards, fluttered to the ground.

"Look, what's that?" Gwen bent down to pick it up.

"At the moment, I don't care what it is." Ricki looked around, frantically.

"I ... I think this is for you." said Gwen after she had read the first few lines.

"What? Show me." Ricki tore the paper out of her friend's hand.

Diablo's owner's eyes widened and she tried to keep her hands from trembling as she read the scribbled writing:

If you want to see your horse again, come to the Echo Lake parking lot at 2:00. Bring Jake with you. Don't say anything to anyone. No police, or I'll turn your horse into salami.

Ricki pressed her eyes shut for a moment to gather her thoughts.

"What does it say? Come on, let me read it, too." Gwen held out her hand. Ricki just stared at her and laughed nervously.

"No, it's not necessary," she lied, completely unbelievably. "Apparently someone is playing a joke with Diablo. It just says where I can pick him up. Just a stupid trick." As she spoke these words, she crumpled up the paper and shoved it in her pants pocket, as though she didn't care whether she saved it or not.

"Oh, great, then let's go and get him. I bet Diablo already misses you."

"No, no. I ... uh ... I think it's better if you wait here. I'll go get him, and then –"

Gwen frowned.

"Ricki, what are you talking about? That's total nonsense. What's really going on?"

The girl bit her lips.

"I ... I can't tell you, or something terrible could happen to Diablo ... What time is it?"

Gwen looked at her watch.

"One fifteen."

"Then I have to go. Please, Gwen, don't say anything about the note to the others."

"But ..."

"Please! Diablo's life depends on it!"

Gwen struggled with what she'd just been asked, but finally she agreed.

"Okay, but promise me that you'll be careful, and call me every ten minutes, okay?"

"Yeah, yeah."

"Not yeah, yeah. Promise!" Gwen was adamant.

Not wanting to waste any more time, Ricki acquiesced, then ran off to get Kevin's bike. She started pedaling like mad and had to be careful not to spin out on the ranch's gravel drive. A few minutes later she had reached the road and exhaled deeply, glad to be out of Gwen's sight. Now she could gather her thoughts.

Cooper! It can only have been Cooper! I knew it!

It was clear that he wanted revenge against her and Jake. After all, she and the stableman were the reason why he had been arrested and why Diablo had been taken from him.

"Oh, what am I going to do? What am I going to do?" stammered Ricki to herself. She was dizzy with fear and had no idea what would happen next.

Suddenly she remembered the horse transporter she had seen on the driveway going toward the road.

That was him, she realized. *He drove Diablo away right in front of my eyes.* At that moment, it all became clear to her.

And there was something else that became clear: Cooper hadn't been joking about horses and salami. He had meant it when he threatened to do something horrible to Diablo.

Ricki knew that the first thing she should do was inform her parents, but she also knew that they would call the police immediately. That could mean she would never see her Diablo alive again.

The only person with whom she would have been able to talk to about this threat was Carlotta. She would have known how to fix everything. But Carlotta couldn't help her now. Ricki sobbed, and then tried to get herself under control so she could think clearly, but her thoughts were doing somersaults in her head.

She pulled the note out of her pocket again, so that she could reread Cooper's instructions.

"... Bring Jake with you."

Jake ... No! With his heart condition, she just couldn't risk involving him in this mess. She had to think of a reason why he wasn't with her.

Ricki hid her face in her hands.

She was all alone with this burden.

She was afraid for Diablo ... and she was terrified to meet up with Cooper.

"Dear God, help me. I don't know what to do," she prayed quietly to herself. Then she got back on Kevin's bike and started off in the direction of Echo Lake.

***

Frank Cooper had come to Mercy Ranch disguised in sun glasses and a toupee, passing himself off as an interested visitor, without knowing exactly how he was going to get to that hated horse.

However, when Eleanor Highland had allowed her emotions to run away with her, and all the visitors were listening to her intently, he seized the opportunity to get the horse from the paddock, unnoticed, and to lead him through the adjacent woods to his transporter, where he loaded him and drove away.

He then put him in an old shed at a deserted farmhouse, a few miles from Mercy Ranch.

Grinning evilly, he put a hackamore on top of the paddock halter and snaffle and attached it so tightly that it caused Diablo pain.

"You're going to obey me," he hissed. "And if you're thinking about kicking me, you'd better think it over carefully. I have no problem pulling that thing even tighter. Come on, you stupid beast!" He pulled roughly on the reins and Diablo followed him meekly, afraid that the pain across his sensitive nose would get even worse.

Now Cooper sat, almost invisible, behind some bushes at Echo Lake, directly across from the parking lot to which he had commanded Ricki and Jake to go.

A glance at his watch showed him that the time he had given Ricki would be up in ten minutes, and he kept looking over at the parking lot through binoculars.

"You'll come," he whispered softly, as though talking to Ricki. "I know you'll come. You would do *anything* for that miserable animal."

***

"Super!"

"Terrific!"

"They're fabulous!"

The audience clapped enthusiastically after Josh and his friends gave their exhibition.

"That's the way I'd like to be able to ride."

"It's so cool."

Kevin stood at the fence with his friends, and nodded with respect.

"Your boyfriend is really a terrific rider," he said to Lillian in admiration. She turned a little red with pride. Then he started looking around.

"It's too bad Ricki missed it. Where is she? I haven't seen her for a while. We should be saddling Sharazan and Diablo for the children's rides." He frowned, annoyed. "Have any of you seen her?"

Everyone, except for Gwen, shook their head.

The girl took a deep breath and tried to act innocent.

"Oh, I forgot. Ah ... um ... Kevin, Ricki rode home on Diablo," she said, quickly crossing her fingers behind her back. She hated to lie to anyone, but she had promised her friend she wouldn't tell anyone.

Kevin whirled around.

"She WHAT?!"

Gwen coughed lightly. "She rode home."

"That can't be. She wouldn't just ride off without saying anything."

"But she told me." She was beginning to regret having said anything.

"Did she at least say why she was riding home?"

Gwen shrugged her shoulders. "I thought you would know."

"No, I don't know. Darn it, we promised to take the kids for rides, and now I'm left holding the bag. Thanks, Ricki. That's just great."

Gwen intervened.

"Oh, come on, it isn't that bad. If you want, I'll saddle Black Jack."

"I thought he only lets you ride him."

Gwen grinned.

"Yes, well, I told you that a long time ago. Now he's fine if someone else is sitting in the saddle, especially if I'm leading him. It'll be okay, don't worry."

"Then, let's get going."

"Oh, I forgot. Granny has my saddle in the car." Gwen slapped her hand against her forehead in dismay.

"We'll find something in the tack room that will fit Black Jack," replied Kevin, and they both ran over to the stable.

When Kevin went into the tack room, he pointed to Diablo's saddle, which was still hanging on the wall, unused.

"I thought you said that Ricki had ridden home?" he asked, confused.

"She did, but without her saddle," Gwen claimed, realizing that she was digging herself deeper and deeper into her lies.

"Hmmm, that's weird. And also without her snaffle, it looks like, doesn't it?" Kevin sensed that Gwen was lying to him. "I don't think you're telling me the truth, Gwen. If we didn't have to give the kids rides right now, I'd get to the bottom of this and find out what's really going on with Ricki."

Gwen turned bright red, but said nothing. Then she glanced secretly at her watch and saw that Ricki, despite her promise, hadn't called once.

"Take Diablo's saddle and gear," Kevin said, coolly. "He and Black Jack are about the same size."

Gwen nodded hastily. "Okay. Then let's go and get the horses."

She ran outside quickly, to avoid any more questions from Kevin. Ricki's boyfriend just stared after her. Something was wrong with the story Gwen had told him, and he was going to find out what it was. The thing that really hurt was that Gwen, and apparently Ricki, didn't trust him, otherwise his girlfriend would have told him herself what was bothering her. The fact that she was probably in some kind of trouble was becoming crystal clear to him.

***

Diablo stood in the tiny shed and kept turning around nervously. He didn't have enough room to do anything else. He kept raising his head and listening intently, trying to hear something, but it was abnormally silent around him. Upset, he snorted through his nostrils and whinnied so loudly that it shook his whole body.

Where was Ricki? Why had this stranger brought him here?

Stranger?

The memory of a long forgotten time awoke in Diablo. This angry person wasn't a stranger to him at all. He had

106

hurt him before, beat him and tied him up too tightly with a sharp bit in his mouth, leaving him standing for hours in his stall. Then Ricki had freed him and his painful mouth had had time to heal.

Where was Ricki?! Why wasn't she here?

He didn't want to be here. He wanted to go back to Sharazan and the paddock behind the ranch.

The black horse threw his head back and kicked out with his hind legs, but he didn't hit the boards, he hit a cement foundation to which the wood was bolted.

When he tried to put his foot down again, he felt a sharp pain in his ankle.

Diablo whinnied again in the hope that Ricki would hear him, but the world was silent all around him.

Resigned, he let his head sink. His leg hurt and he tried, as much as possible, not to put any weight on it.

He kept licking his muzzle and then the iron bar that went from one wall to the other over his head. He had an unquenchable thirst, but Cooper hadn't even put a bucket of water in the shed.

Diablo didn't understand why he was here.

If only Ricki would come ...

***

Gwen led her black horse behind Sharazan, around and around the paddock, letting the chatter of the children flow over Black Jack's back and to her. She was worried about Ricki, who had not kept her promise to call.

Kevin hadn't said a word to her. He was furious with Gwen for lying. Stubbornly, he looked straight ahead. The hour that had been scheduled for the children's rides had long expired, and the line of kids waiting to ride wasn't getting any shorter.

107

It was unbelievable how many people were still walking around Mercy Ranch in the afternoon, and Sean as well as Kieran had their hands full giving out information about fostering a horse or adopting one of the horses on the ranch.

***

Carlotta would have been very happy about the events at the ranch, but she wasn't able to enjoy any of it. She lay in her bed in the intensive care unit at the hospital, connected to various machines, her head wrapped thickly in bandages, a nurse at her bedside.

Caroline and Mrs. Highland stood outside her room. They had been staring through the glass at their dear friend for hours, but Carlotta hadn't moved an eyelash since the operation.

"Do you think she'll make it, Mrs. Highland?" Kevin's mother asked softly, looking through completely exhausted eyes.

"Call me Eleanor," came the reply, instead of an answer.

"Caroline," Kevin's mother tried to smile. "I wish with all my heart that she comes through this. But the doctor ... he didn't sound very hopeful."

Mrs. Highland swallowed and held her gaze on her friend.

"I'll eat my hat if she doesn't survive," she said, but Caroline wasn't sure that Eleanor really believed what she said. "Carlotta has never given up in her whole life, regardless of what happened, and I am convinced that she will fight. Carlotta Mancini won't let a stupid tumor finish her off."

Caroline looked to the side and noticed that two tears were rolling down Mrs. Highland's cheeks.

She sensed that Mrs. Highland wasn't as strong as she pretended to be. Instinctively, she put her arm around Carlotta's best friend.

"You should go home and rest a little," said the nurse as they left Carlotta's room. "At the moment, there's nothing you can do. Mrs. Mancini will sleep for the next two days."

Eleanor nodded absently, and then she said to Caroline, "Come on, let's go. She's right. You're so exhausted, you could sleep standing up."

After one more look at their friend, the two women left the unit. They would come back the next day and the day after that as well. They would stand behind the glass when Carlotta woke up, and they would do everything possible to help her back to her normal life again.

If Carlotta survived, however, according to the doctor it was quite possible that she would be very different from the woman they had known ... whatever that meant.

***

The closer Ricki got to Echo Lake, the wilder her heart beat. Now she was standing all alone in the parking lot, looking around, scared. There was no one to be seen.

Had she read it wrong? Was she supposed to go someplace else?

She pulled out the note one more time and read it yet again. No, there it was; *Echo Lake parking lot.*

But why was she here alone?

Nervously, she rubbed her forehead.

What should she do now? Wait? If so, for how long?

What did Diablo's kidnapper have planned?

She stood in the middle of the parking lot for ten minutes holding on to Kevin's bike.

"I'm here," she called out suddenly. "I'm alone. Where are you? Where is Diablo?" Ricki's voice sounded shaky.

She turned around in a circle, but didn't see Cooper anywhere.

The girl panicked. What if he doesn't come at all? Then she would never find out where he had taken her beloved horse. She wondered if Diablo was all right. She knew Cooper well enough to know that he wouldn't hesitate to beat Diablo or do other awful things to him.

"I'm here," she called out again, a little louder.

"I can see that! Don't yell."

Ricki turned around quickly.

She hadn't seen Cooper coming at all, and now that he was walking toward her, her knees turned to pudding and, for a brief moment, she thought she was going to fall down.

"Where is Diablo?" she asked, her voice hoarse, and stepped back a few feet as the man came to stand right in front of her. "Where is he? Where did you take him?"

Cooper grinned nastily.

"You'd like to know, wouldn't you?" Then his coal-black eyes filled with anger. "Where's the old man?"

Ricki started to tremble.

"He ... He couldn't come with me."

Cooper's eyes narrowed into slits.

"You're lying."

Ricki turned red and then pale. She thought quickly.

"N-no. He's ... sick. His heart ... He's been sick for a week. He can't get up... He's in bed." Ricki took a breath. "Please, Mr. Cooper ... Where is Diablo?" she stammered.

"Do you know what it's like to be locked up? Imprisoned in a small room, with no one nearby you can talk to? And just because a stupid girl and an old stable groom thought they had to save a horse. Do you know what you did to me?" Cooper came dangerously close.

"You tortured him," breathed Ricki, taking two steps backward.

110

"Tortured!" He laughed coldly before his rage toward her became evident in his eyes. "A filthy beast, not worth anything."

"Diablo isn't a filthy beast."

"Shut up!" Cooper took a step forward, but Ricki threw the bike at him and tried to run away.

Diablo's former owner stumbled.

"If you run away now, you'll never see your nag again!" he screamed after her, and Ricki slowed down.

"Look over here," yelled Cooper, furiously. "Look over here closely."

Ricki stood still and looked back over her shoulder in fear. It almost killed her when she saw what the hateful man suddenly pulled from behind his back and waved over his head like a trophy.

"Oh, no!" The girl felt sick to her stomach. For a moment, she closed her eyes, and then she walked back, one slow step at a time.

"I knew that'd convince you," Cooper grinned, and threw Diablo's long mane, which he had cut off sloppily, at Ricki's feet.

"Oh, no ... where is he?" the girl sobbed and sank to her knees. Trembling, she stroked the long silky horsehair that had been Diablo's pride. "You ... you're crazy!" Her voice broke.

"Oh, yes! Crazy!" Cooper nodded. "That's what they all said. Come with me." Roughly, he grabbed her arm, pulled her up, and then shoved her in front of him. "You go crazy when you're locked up. Get going. Move!" He pushed her behind some bushes to a path hidden in the woods where he had left his car.

There he opened the trunk and took out two rags.

111

Ricki's eyes widened in fear.

"What are you going to do?"

"You'll see soon enough."

Without another word, he pulled her arms back and tied her hands together with one of the rags.

"No!" whimpered Ricki. "Please don't!"

"Be quiet, you stable rat!"

With the other rag he blindfolded Ricki, then forced her into the passenger seat and slammed the door shut.

"We're going to take a little trip."

"Where are you taking me?" Ricki's whole body shook.

"If you're quiet and you shut up, then nothing will happen to you," replied Cooper, in a calm, almost friendly voice.

"Are you taking me to Diablo?"

"I told you to shut up!" Cooper started the car, and Ricki hardly dared to breathe. Then she remembered that she was supposed to call Gwen, and she regretted very much that she hadn't done so. Now her friends had absolutely no idea where she was. She could only hope that Gwen had caught a brief glance at the note that Cooper had written before Ricki grabbed it away from her. That would at least give them a clue to her whereabouts. But even if that were true, there was no clue to where Cooper was now taking her.

Ricki let her head sink to her chest.

It's over! she thought with despair.

No one would look for her. She had made Gwen promise not to tell anyone, because she was afraid that something would happen to Diablo, and if she knew her friend, Gwen wouldn't say anything. Ricki couldn't hope for any help. She was alone with this torturer and she had never been so frightened in her life.

112

She didn't know how long they had been driving when Cooper stopped the car.

While they were driving, Ricki had calmed down a bit. The man couldn't do anything to her as he was driving. But now that they had come to the place he was taking her, her heart began to thump wildly again.

Cooper was in control of her, and since she didn't know what he was planning, she was terrified.

"Get out," he ordered her and pulled her out of the car. Then he pushed her to walk in front of him, and because she couldn't see, she stumbled often.

Suddenly, a door creaked, and Ricki didn't feel any more stones under her feet; she was on a smooth surface. Cooper must have brought her to a house. But where?

After a few yards and steps that she had to stumble up blindly, Cooper pushed open a door and shoved her forward roughly.

With a scream, she fell and landed hard on the floor.

Cooper ripped off the blindfold, and Ricki found herself in a dark room that was barely lit and sparsely furnished. Everything was dusty and dirty, and it was clear that no one had lived here for a long time.

"Do you like it?" Cooper asked, his words dripping with sarcasm. "This is a luxury apartment compared to the place I was locked up in."

Ricki gulped. "Where is Diablo?"

Cooper turned bright red and Ricki was afraid that he was going to explode.

"Diablo! It's always Diablo!" he yelled. "Forget that miserable beast."

"What ... what are you going to do with him?"

The man laughed. "You'll find that out soon enough."

Then he turned around and walked to the door. But before he left the room, he warned, "Don't even think about screaming. It could have bad consequences for you." He left the room quickly and slammed the door shut. The key grated harshly in the lock.

"Please," Ricki called out. "My hands. They hurt so much. Please untie them!"

Cooper walked away, paying no attention to Ricki's pleas.

"Untie me!" she screamed as loudly as she could, somewhere between panic, rage, and fear.

Then she heard him come back.

At the sound of the key, the door flung open, and an angry Cooper stood in front of her.

"I told you not to scream!" he said, dangerously calm. Then he reached for the blindfold and waved it in front of her face. "One more sound, and I will gag you with this. Understand?"

Ricki nodded almost unnoticeably. She didn't want to be gagged. She wouldn't be able to stand that.

"All right, then." And he was gone.

The girl let herself fall sidewise onto the floor and sobbed. Her hands and arms hurt, but it hurt her more not to know what was happening to Diablo. She wondered if that devil Cooper had done something even more terrible to him than cutting off his mane.

Ricki was still holding tightly to the long hairs of her horse.

"At least one part of you is here with me," she sobbed softly to herself. "Diablo, I was so stupid. I should have gone to the police. Now we don't stand a chance. Cooper can do whatever he wants with us and no one will know. Kevin ... help me ... please, Kevin!"

She cried bitterly, but when she had no more tears to cry she suddenly remembered that she still had her cell phone. Cooper must have forgotten that almost all teenagers carry a cell phone.

If she managed to get to the phone in her pants pocket, and could untie her hands, then she could call the ranch and ...

Her last glimmer of hope disappeared when she looked down. Where her phone normally peeked out of her pocket, there was nothing. She must have lost it somewhere.

Chapter 8

Sean sat in Carlotta's office with Caroline and Mrs. Highland as they gave him the latest news about his boss's condition.

"It's still the same," said Caroline wearily. "The doctors aren't very hopeful. She should have had the operation sooner. Her doctor said he couldn't raise our hopes, and, even if she survives she won't be the same. Can you imagine that, Sean? Carlotta not the same woman? It's a horrible thought."

Sean clenched his teeth.

He was about to answer but just then someone knocked on the door.

"Not now," he said, louder than he wanted to, but Gwen had already stuck her head in the doorway.

"Please, Granny, I have to talk with you."

Mrs. Highland rolled her eyes. She didn't feel like dealing with any teenagers right now.

"Can't we talk later?"

Gwen came in and shook her head.

"No. I'm sorry, but it's important. Please!"

Eleanor got up with a sigh.

"I'll be right back," she said, and went with Gwen to the kitchen.

"I don't know how to begin," groaned Gwen, feeling overwhelmingly guilty. But she couldn't keep quiet any longer and so she told her grandmother about Ricki and Diablo's disappearance.

"That's unbelievable. Gwendolyn, I thought you were smarter than that. Why didn't you tell somebody?"

"I promised her I wouldn't. And anyway, you weren't here!"

"Sean Devlin was here."

Gwen nodded. "Yeah, but I don't know him at all. I didn't know if I could trust him," she replied, defending her decision.

"If Carlotta has employed him as her manager, then there is no reason why you shouldn't trust him," Eleanor Highland paused. "But I do understand your motives."

"Thank you!" Gwen threw her arms around her grandmother. "I'm so glad I could finally tell someone. Granny, I'm so afraid for Ricki. What if something's happened to her? Then it's my fault, isn't it?"

"No, my love," her grandmother said softly, shaking her head. "Ricki should have turned to her parents and the police. She shouldn't have tried to be a hero all by herself."

"But what should we do now? She said I shouldn't tell anyone because if I did something might happen to Diablo."

Mrs. Highland looked down at her granddaughter gravely.

117

"As much as I love horses, Gwen, and as wonderful as I think Diablo is, Ricki is more important. Come with me." Determined, she marched back to Carlotta's office, pulling Gwen with her.

"Caroline ... Mr. Devlin, we have another problem," she said as she entered. "It looks as if we aren't going to be spared anything today."

***

"What's the matter with you?" Lillian asked Kevin, who was sitting on the bench next to the hot dog grill with a scowl on his face. "Can I offer you something to eat? Cake? Hot dog? Muffin? Salad?"

"No thanks. I'm not hungry."

Lillian looked at him intently. "You, not hungry? You must be sick."

"Worried is more like it."

"Is it because of Ricki?"

"Yeah. Can you tell me why she just left without saying anything?"

Lillian shook her head no. "Gwen said –"

"Don't mention Gwen." Kevin snorted. "She's lying!"

"Are you serious?"

"Yes. Or do you have a plausible explanation why Ricki would ride home on Diablo without her saddle and snaffle? That's ridiculous."

"How about calling her at home, or on her cell phone?"

"I already did, but nobody answers either phone. And her parents went away for the weekend, I think."

"What about calling Cathy or Oliver? The two of them are probably at the Sulais' stable," suggested Lillian.

"Cathy is home with her sprained ankle and I already tried Oliver. He's out with Miz Lizzy and the foal."

"Darn!"

"You can say that again!" Kevin sat up straighter and stretched. "I have a really bad feeling."

"Then go to Sean. Maybe he knows something."

Kevin nodded slowly.

"Yeah." He got up. "And if not, then I'm going to ride over to the Sulais with Sharazan and see if I can find Ricki." He looked around. "It's almost over here, anyway. The few visitors that are left will probably be leaving soon." He ran off toward the house.

Josh came riding up to Lillian on Cherish. Following their performance, he and his friends had spent the rest of the afternoon at the ranch, and had allowed kids to sit on their horses and be led around the grounds.

"Hey, here is the most beautiful girl of all," he said and looked at Lillian with love. "Is everything okay?"

"With me, yes, but Kevin's all upset." She told her boyfriend about Ricki and Diablo's mysterious disappearance and about Gwen's strange tale.

"That sounds really weird." Josh raised his eyebrows. "And now she's gone and Kevin wants ... oh, look, here he comes."

Lillian turned around. " ... and with Gwen. They must have made up."

Kevin came up to Lillian and Josh and said, "Ricki took my bike, and she must have ridden to Echo Lake."

"Why?" asked Josh.

"Because ... because someone was waiting for her there to bring her to Diablo."

"What do you mean, 'bring her to Diablo'? I thought she rode home on him." Lillian didn't understand until Gwen told them the truth.

119

While Gwen was relieving her guilty conscience, Cheryl joined them. She listened silently.

"I wonder if it could be that Cooper guy," she said.

"Cooper? Who is that?" Eleanor's granddaughter wanted to know.

"He's in prison, isn't he?" Kevin looked at Lillian, and then he turned to Cheryl. "What made you think of him?"

"Well, because yesterday, as we were riding home, a car passed us and Ricki acted really strange. She thought she recognized the driver and that it was Diablo's former owner – and she said that she was afraid he would do something to Diablo."

"Oh, no! Not Frank Cooper, that miserable excuse for a human being. I wouldn't put anything past him." Kevin didn't even want to think about the possibilities. "If it turns out that he's behind all this, then we can only hope we find Ricki and Diablo in time, before he really lets his anger loose."

"You think we should look for Ricki?"

"Of course," Kevin emphatically responded. "What else?"

"My grandmother wants to get the police involved," commented Gwen.

"Yeah, but by the time they get around to doing something, who knows what will happen? I'd rather depend on myself. I'm going to ride to Echo Lake. Who's coming with me?"

"Everyone. Of course." Lillian was excited to be part of it all, that is, until Josh took both her hands in his and looked directly into her eyes.

"Oh, no, sweetheart, you're staying here."

"No, I'm not," she protested, but Josh shook his head decisively.

"Yes, you are."

"And why should I?"

"First of all, because you're not fit enough yet, as far as the riding is concerned ..."

"That's ridiculous! I –"

"And because someone has to stay here and help out. We can't leave Sean alone here. After all, there are still some visitors left, and someone has to tell Sean so he can let the police know about Cooper."

"Terrific." Lillian sounded disappointed.

"And you don't have your horse here, anyway."

She sighed. "Those are the only reasons I'll accept."

"So, who's coming?" Kevin asked again.

"Everyone."

"Gwen, Cheryl, come on. Let's get our horses saddled." The three were already on their way to the stable.

Josh, on the other hand, rode over to his friends, and not three minutes later the seven Western riders and their horses were ready and waiting for Kevin and the girls.

"Okay, let's go." Kevin said.

"Good luck!" Kieran and Hal, who were staying behind with Lillian, called as they all rode off.

***

"Where are the others?" Sean asked about fifteen minutes later, when Lillian finally found him and told him about their search. He was furious and scolded her angrily.

"You guys are always taking risks without thinking them over first. Don't you all realize how dangerous this could be? Why couldn't you talk this over with me or another adult?"

"But there are ten of them," Lillian defended Kevin and her boyfriend. However, Sean just snorted and ran back to the house. It was just one thing after another today.

Ricki's wrists hurt. She had kept trying to loosen the tie that bound her, so that she could free herself, but the more she pulled, the tighter it got. Meanwhile, she had almost no feeling left in her hands.

She got up from the mattress awkwardly and walked to the window. Outside was an old wooden shutter that was partially shut, so she could only see through two tiny slits. Although she couldn't see much, she thought hard about whether she recognized the area, but she had no idea where she was.

Everything was eerily quiet. No noises could be heard.

She wondered if Cooper had driven away, but she hadn't heard any motor.

Was he still in the house? That he was somewhere nearby was a horrible thought.

And what about Diablo?

Ricki bit her lips until they bled to keep herself from screaming. She would never get over it if something happened to her horse.

Feeling weak, she leaned her forehead on the windowpane.

"Where are you?" she asked softly, as though her black horse were somewhere close by and could hear her.

Suddenly, her head shot up.

What was that? She listened intently.

There. There it was again. It was very muffled, but the noise she heard was one she knew all too well.

It was definitely hooves thundering against a wooden wall.

Diablo?

Inside Ricki, a storm broke out.

Was it possible that Cooper had brought her somewhere close to her horse? If that was true, then she just had to free herself!

She started searching the dark room. It had to be possible to find something that would help her loosen or cut the tie. But Cooper had apparently removed anything that could have helped.

A whinny! And so loud!

Ricki's blood froze.

She had heard Diablo whinnying like that only once before! It was when he had been locked in the riding academy stable and it caught on fire ... It was a whinny caused by panic!

It drove the girl almost crazy to be locked up, helpless, while she thought of Cooper and the terrible things that he could do, or, heaven forbid, was doing to her horse. She had to save Diablo from his abuser again, no matter what the cost!

As Ricki thought about the danger Diablo was in, her fear turned to rage against the man who was obviously without conscience.

She forced herself to calm down and think.

If Cooper was with Diablo – and she was certain he was, considering the way her horse sounded – then at least he wasn't anywhere near her, and that meant she had to free herself and leave her prison now. She knew she wouldn't have a better chance.

"Don't be afraid, my sweetie, I'm going to manage it. I don't know yet how, but I will, and I'm going to get you out of there, wherever you are. I promise you," she whispered, her voice hoarse.

Again she scanned the room for something to use to free herself. When she spied an old wooden chair in the far corner, opposite the mattress, she suddenly got an idea. With one foot she pushed the chair in front of the window, got up onto it, and then kicked at the window.

***

Kevin and his friends arrived at Echo Lake. With fear in their hearts they rode to the parking lot.

Kevin had grown silent the last few yards, and his fear for Ricki's safety was written on his face.

Josh, who was riding next to him, observed him silently. He knew what it meant to be afraid for his girlfriend. When Lillian lay in the hospital after the accident, he had been so afraid she would never recover the use of her legs.

As they had reached the entrance to the parking lot, Kevin's heart stood still and he brought Sharazan to an abrupt halt. There, on the ground, lay his bike, in the exact spot it had landed after Ricki had thrown it at Cooper.

Slowly Kevin slid down from the saddle and handed Gwen his reins. Then he stumbled to his bike and knelt down next to it.

"She was here," he said, his voice shaky. "She was here, and something terrible happened. I can feel it. ... Oh no, what are we going to do now? She could be anywhere!"

Josh, who had dismounted too, stood next to him with Cherish and looked around.

Suddenly he led his horse two steps to the side, bent down and picked up a long, thin strand of black horsehair.

Silently he held it out to Kevin.

"Diablo!"

"Oh, whoa, what is this?" Lex burst out. A vet student and Josh's friend, Lex leaned across the saddle of his black-and-white piebald, Charon, to get a better look, and said in disbelief, "If I hadn't been here, I wouldn't have believed

124

it. It can only be Cooper. No one else would be capable of kidnapping Ricki. He knew that she would go with him immediately if he held some of Diablo's mane in front of her nose. What a piece of pond scum!"

The other Western riders, all of them strong young men, looked at one another gravely as they each thought hard about what to do. Their usual high spirits had disappeared.

Kevin picked up his bike absently and pushed it to the side of the parking lot. Then he took up the reins of his horse.

"We have to look for her!"

"But where should we start?" asked Pepe. "If he took her with him and drove for miles, then we'll never find her. How could we? There are no other clues, are there?"

Gwen shook her head.

"Maybe we should call the police and let them take over finding her," commented Andre. "This is a kidnapping, after all, and they know how to handle these things."

His friends agreed, but Kevin shook his head stubbornly.

"I can't just ride back home and wait for the police to get started."

"But Kevin, it's senseless to just start riding without a plan, without even knowing which direction to go," replied Andre, trying to be practical.

"You don't have to come with me. As far as I'm concerned, you can all go back home!" Kevin was getting more frantic, and it showed in his voice.

"Stay calm, buddy!" Josh put his hand on Kevin's shoulder. "Of course we'll help you look, but at least let's be thorough. We have to try to think like Cooper in order to figure out where he could have gone."

"Oh, that's just great. Can you think like a crazy person? I can't!"

125

Josh didn't even try to reply.

"Let's think about what's nearby, where he could have brought her," he said instead.

"Who says that he brought her somewhere nearby? If I wanted to hide someone so no one would find them, I would go far away," Kevin said.

"See!" replied Josh after thinking for a moment. "That's exactly the point. I think that he thinks everyone will assume she's far away, and that's exactly why he took her somewhere near here."

"How stupid would that be?"

"That wouldn't be stupid, Kevin, it would be clever," said Lex, and nodded in admiration. "Josh, you're a genius!"

"Cooper is, at least as far as this is concerned, unpredictable, I think," commented Kevin.

"You think or you know?"

"Oh, please, stop trying to analyze this." Kevin's nerves were ready to explode.

"Listen, Kevin. No matter where he brought Ricki, we can only ride a few more miles on the horses. Any farther, and we'll have to use a car. But you try to find someone who is hidden somewhere in a building. Cooper won't have put up any signs or have a cell phone handy, so we can't ask him where Ricki is."

"Oh, please, Lex, just stop talking. I know all that."

Josh had been following the conversation carefully, when he suddenly said, "Wait a minute. Cell phone – that gives me an idea. Kevin, does Ricki have her phone with her? Does she usually leave it on?"

"Usually, yes. But she's not answering. I've tried a million times to call her. She –"

"No, no. That's not what I mean. But we could ... wait a minute!"

Somewhat confused, the riders regarded their friend, who had rapidly pulled out his phone and was now holding it to his ear.

"Lillian!" He was almost yelling into the phone. "Lillian ... What? ... No, I don't have any time. Listen. Go to Carlotta's office right away ... No! Listen to what I'm saying. Go to Carlotta's office and sit down in front of the computer. If Sean isn't there, do it anyway. It's an emergency and I'm sure that he wouldn't – What? He's mad? Whatever! Now, go to the home page that I'm going to give you now, and then do the following ..." Quickly he explained a few details to her, and then finished by saying, "Call me immediately if you find anything." He took a deep breath. "If all goes the way I plan, then we'll know in five minutes where Ricki is. Assuming, that is, that she has her cell phone with her."

"Cell phone locating," said Pepe with a grin, "I forgot that you have a connection who can do that kind of stuff. Naughty, naughty, Josh, but I should have thought of it myself."

"And what if she doesn't have it with her anymore?" asked Gwen softly.

"Then at least we'll have the general direction, I hope!"

***

Cooper stood in front of Diablo's shed with a mean, ugly look on his face, and observed him through squinted eyes.

"You are such an ugly beast without your mane," he spat at him in an angry whisper. Then he slapped the horse hard with his open palm on his sensitive muzzle, making Diablo roll his eyes, jerk his head back, and whinny in pain.

"Don't you dare try to bite me ever again," he screamed at the black horse, threatening him with his fist. "You really are the worst animal on the planet! The very worst!" he added with emphasis. "You're just as crazy as your owner!" He snorted derisively. "Owner ... ha! That makes me laugh! That little stable rat stole you! Took advantage of me! But that's over!" He laughed contemptuously. "She'd have to be a moron to fall into a trap because of you, and to believe that I would just let the two of you go. Stupid, really, very, very stupid!"

Cooper stood in front of the horse and seemed to be thinking something over.

"You're thirsty? Of course, you're thirsty. Wait!" He bent down and picked up the bucket at his feet. Then he filled it from an old rusty faucet and came back to the horse.

Diablo looked thirstily at the cool water. He would have given anything to be able to drink that wonderful water in long strong gulps, but Cooper wasn't thinking about relieving the horse's thirst at all.

He raised the bucket and threw the water directly into Diablo's face, breaking out into insane laughter.

"Enjoy!" he yelled and threw the empty bucket against the wall, leaving the shed with quick steps. Now he was going to take care of the girl.

Diablo didn't know what had happened to him. This horrible man was treating him much worse than before. He sensed that he hadn't yet reached the limits of what he could endure, and that Cooper would make him suffer even more than he already had. Diablo knew he had to break out of this cage so that he wouldn't have to undergo any more torture at the hands of this cruel man ... And there was something else: Instinctively he felt that Ricki was also in danger. But what could he do locked up here?

128

Cautiously, he tried putting weight on his hind leg. It didn't bother him any more. He moved in a circle two or three times to try it out, and when nothing hurt him, he thundered against the back wall with his hooves. He whinnied shrilly as he kicked out again and again. Finally the wood began to splinter.

***

Ricki stood with her back to the broken window, her face bright red and sweaty, and rubbed the knot carefully across a piece of broken glass that jutted out. She hoped that she wouldn't cut herself. She kept stopping and listening outside. Diablo was storming wildly in his prison, but she didn't hear anything from Cooper.

Ricki's fear for her horse grew every second that went by. The way Diablo sounded, he must be in a terrible situation. She wondered if Cooper were torturing him again, as he had back when he owned him. Was he beating him? Sticking a pitchfork into him?

The girl couldn't stand thinking about what the man was capable of doing.

She continued to rub the rag across the broken glass, and since the knot wasn't very thick, she managed to cut through it in a relatively short time. Then she was able to free herself.

Groaning, she massaged her painful red wrists, and slowly life returned to her numb hands. When the blood had finally circulated enough, Ricki felt as though thousands of tiny needles were pricking her skin, but she didn't have a chance to feel sorry for herself. She knew that she didn't have much time to escape her captor. Sooner or later, he would stand in the doorway, and Ricki didn't even want to think about what would happen then. She had to find a way to leave the house without Cooper discovering her. After that, she was sure that everything else would fall into place.

***

"Did he get it?" Josh stared at Kevin while he pressed his cell phone to his ear. "Okay, great! That's what I thought! Then we can get going. See you later, Lily, and cross your fingers for us. And, thanks, sweetheart."

His friends looked at him expectantly, and Kevin's hands began to tremble a little. "So, people, I think we can get going." Josh nodded and winked at Kevin. "It looks as though my theory wasn't far off."

"Where is she?"

"Where she is, I can't say yet. But I do know where her cell phone is." Josh swung himself up into the saddle. "There's a rundown farm near the hunting lodge."

Kevin's head whipped around.

"You mean that old deserted place that's near the edge of the woods, where the fence around the paddock is collapsed?"

"Exactly!" Josh nodded. "It's pretty isolated. We rarely ever go near it."

"That's the place we found Ricki's dog." Kevin looked at his watch.

"It'll take us about forty-five minutes to get there," guessed Josh.

"We should tell somebody at the ranch what's going on," said Cheryl. "Maybe Sean can drive there in the car, or send someone."

"Do what you want," complained Kevin. He wasn't going to waste any more time talking. "I'm gonna get going. Sharazan is rested, so we'll make it there in less than forty-five!" And he galloped off on his roan.

"That guy is getting on my nerves," groaned Pepe. "Is he always like that ... going off half-cocked all the time?"

"Well, sort of. Actually, though, he's usually pretty relaxed," answered Cheryl. "Does anyone mind if I call Sean?"

"No, go ahead. And then we'll take off after Kevin," replied Josh.

Less than two minutes later, the kids mounted up again and chased after their friend. They all felt pretty much the same as Kevin. The faster they could help Ricki and Diablo, the better!

Chapter 9

Ricki shook the doorknob as gently as possible, hoping
that the old lock would give way, but it didn't budge. The
massive door was made of hardwood, and there was no
way to break it open, even if she threw herself against it.
She had to find another means of escape.

Very carefully she opened the broken window and, with her
heart pounding, she undid the latch holding the shutters. With
a loud creak, she pushed one shutter forward a little, which
allowed her to see outside, even though the opening was narrow.

"So this is where he brought me," Ricki murmured when,
finally, she could recognize something. *A popular spot to
hide someone,* she thought cynically. She remembered how
Rosie's unscrupulous owner had left the dog tied up here for
who knows how long. Only after Ricki had called the vet did
she discover that Rosie was pregnant and badly dehydrated
and malnourished.

Then she looked down. It was at least fifteen feet to the ground, much too high for Ricki to jump down. Nevertheless, she didn't have any other option than to climb through the window.

Meanwhile, Diablo was behaving wildly, and Ricki, too, was feeling panicky listening to her horse raging. Desperately she looked outside and tried to figure out in which of the dilapidated sheds Cooper had put Diablo.

He must be over there, she thought, as she suddenly heard a loud crack and saw a puff of dust coming through the slits in the rotted wooden wall of one of the sheds. Almost at the same time, she heard Cooper's steps on the stairs leading to her room.

Ricki whirled around and pressed her body against the wall in fear. What was she going to do? She couldn't jump out of the window and risk breaking a leg. Then it would be all over and she wouldn't be able to help Diablo anymore. On the other hand, she couldn't flee through the door if Cooper came in.

All sorts of ideas rushed wildly through her mind, and she realized that she had only one chance.

Quickly she went back to the window, opened it wide and threw back the shutters with a loud bang. Then she ran over to the door and pressed herself into the corner. All she could do was wait and hope that Cooper would fall for her trick. If not, then –

She had no more time to think about it. The key creaked in the lock, the door flew open, and Cooper stared into the apparently empty room. Only when he had looked twice did he discover the broken window and the open shutters.

Swearing, he ran into the room and looked out the

window. He was puzzled by how Ricki could have escaped from this height.

She took a deep breath.

It's now or never, Ricki thought, and she propelled herself around the open door and ran down the stairs. Only much later did she realize that it would have been better to slam the door behind her and turn the key in the lock than just run away.

But by the time she thought of it, it was too late. Cooper was hot on her heels.

She was already outside when she heard a crash behind her and a scream. Cooper must have stumbled on the stairs and fallen.

Ricki, who had never wished anything bad for anyone up to now, caught herself praying that Cooper had broken a leg so that he couldn't follow her, but her prayer was not answered. The man had gotten back up and was now chasing her again.

"Diablo!" screamed Ricki shrilly. "Diablo!" She wouldn't dream of leaving him behind to hide from Cooper. She was much too afraid that the abusive man would go berserk and take out his fury on her horse.

Finally, she made it across the yard, coming to a standstill in front of the crooked door of the shed. Her knees were shaking.

"Diablo! Diabloooo! Are you in there?" Wildly she fumbled with the wooden bar that ran across the door. It was jammed in tightly and wouldn't budge, no matter how hard she pounded on it.

Ricki sobbed. She was completely exhausted.

Cooper came running out into the yard, but when he saw Ricki's futile attempts to get the shed door open, his steps grew slower, like a lion getting ready to pounce on his prey.

Ricki looked back over her shoulder and shook the door wildly. It was closed and would stay closed if a miracle didn't happen.

Ricki twirled around and then stood in front of the door with her arms stretched out. No! She would not allow Cooper to get near her horse ever again!

"Don't you feel ridiculous?" grinned Cooper, wickedly. "Do you really believe you can stop me from doing what I wanted to do to that beast years ago?" His laughter sounded insane and gave Ricki goose bumps.

"Leave my horse alone!" she screamed at him, her legs almost collapsing.

"It's too bad the old man didn't come with you," Cooper hissed. "I would have liked to have two observers present when the horse finally breathes his last!"

Cooper was only six feet away from Ricki.

Almost pityingly, he smiled at her, and then he lunged at her, grabbed her, and pulled her arm so hard behind her back that she cried out in pain.

"Now you get to watch this spectacle all by yourself. That's not bad either," he panted.

"You're crazy! Insane!" screamed Ricki and tried to kick the man behind her in the legs, but he was much too strong for her to defend herself. She knew she had no chance.

***

Diablo hesitated when he heard Ricki's screams. He twitched his ears and blew through his nostrils.

"No! Nooo!" she yelled. "Leave my horse alone! Owww!"

Ricki is here and she is in danger!

Wild, almost like a scream, his whinny was a challenge to fight. Powerfully he reared up and crashed his hooves onto the wooden door of his shed.

Ricki heard the wood splinter.

"No, Diablo! Don't!" she screamed in fear for her horse. But the horse's hooves thundered against the wood again and again. If he kept that up he might break his legs.

"Diablo, don't do that!" sobbed Ricki as Cooper shoved her back to the house.

"Let him go! If he breaks his neck, it'll just save me a lot of work. Even though it'll spoil your show. Get moving! It won't get any better if you keep trying to stop me!" he yelled at Ricki. "I –"

"Take your hands off her, you miserable maggot!" Kevin's voice suddenly boomed.

More surprised than frightened, Cooper spun around. He could hardly believe what he saw.

Ten determined riders were galloping toward him.

Confused, he stood there staring for a few seconds. Then he pushed Ricki to the ground and took off.

"Come on, boys, let's get him!" shouted Josh. Pepe swung his Stetson above his head like a cowboy in a Wild West movie and galloped faster.

"Ye-ah!" he shouted loudly, preparing to catch the villainous creep. Lex glanced at him with disapproval, but Pepe just grinned back at him.

"Runaway cattle are caught with a lasso, aren't they?" he called out, reaching for his rope, which still hung over his saddle from their performance at Mercy Ranch.

"Yee-haw!" he shouted, swinging the lasso above his head. His friends fanned out with their horses until they made a large galloping circle around Cooper. They gradually made the circle smaller and tighter so the man had no chance of escaping. With a victory cry, Pepe threw the lasso over Cooper's shoulders and tugged at the rope. Cooper was pulled off his feet and remained breathless on the ground. He knew the game was up.

Ricki had taken no time to watch what was happening to Cooper or to wonder how her friends had been able to find her.

Kevin tried to put his arms around her, but the girl shrugged him loose.

"Diablo's going to kill himself! Help me open the door!" And off she ran, back to the shed, Gwen and Kevin right behind her. Cheryl held Black Jack's and Sharazan's reins and breathlessly watched the unplanned performance of the Western riders.

"Diablo stop it! Do you hear me? Stop it!" called Ricki, but her horse was behaving like a wild thing in the shed. "Darn! Why can't we open this thing?"

Kevin pushed her aside.

"Let me try. The latch is totally crooked!" he said. He kicked at the door two or three times as hard as he could, and the wooden beam got a little looser. "It should work now."

Working together, the kids finally managed to get the heavy piece of wood out.

Ricki jerked the door open and Diablo burst outside, over the splintered wood of his prison shed, stumbling to freedom.

"Diablo, calm down, calm down, that's my good boy! Stay! Stand still. Good boy! Stay calm." Ricki put herself in his path and grabbed for his halter, but Diablo was totally spooked, and he tore himself loose and galloped away.

137

"Hold on to him," Ricki managed to say before she fell to the ground.

Gwen jumped to the side instinctively, but Kevin was completely surprised by the horse's breakout. He saw Diablo racing toward him, and just at the last moment the black horse moved to the side and galloped past him.

He was out of control.

Ricki picked herself up and, limping slightly, she leaned shakily against the shed as she watched her horse galloping away.

"I'll bring him back to you. I promise!" called Kevin, and he swung up into Sharazan's saddle without using the stirrups. Before he was even settled into the saddle, Sharazan began galloping after his four-legged friend.

Josh and Lex became aware of the chase.

"Are you all right on your own?" Josh asked Pepe. He nodded and gave the okay sign with his fingers.

"Don't worry," he grinned. "This guy isn't going anywhere. You just worry about getting Ricki's horse back!"

"Okay ... Lex?"

Lex nodded and together the two of them raced after Diablo.

Sharazan was now almost neck and neck with Ricki's horse, but it was impossible for Kevin to reach for Diablo's halter. It was just a little too far away, and at this speed Kevin didn't want to get any closer to the fleeing horse.

Josh and Lex caught up on their horses.

"Trick number seventeen?" called out Josh.

"Yep!" replied Lex, and as though on command, the two riders separated like a fork in the road.

They urged their horses to give their all and actually

managed to shoot past Sharazan and Diablo, on the left and the right. Soon they were half a length ahead.

"Kevin, get behind Diablo," shouted Josh as he and Lex brought their horses together in front of Diablo and blocked his path. Slowly they decreased their speed, so that Diablo fell into a quick trot.

"Now, Kevin!"

The boy understood.

Quickly, he caught up with Ricki's horse and this time he managed to grab hold of his halter.

"Whoa, Diablo! Whoa, boy!" he shouted, completely breathless, and after a few yards, the black horse seemed to have had enough. "You're a good boy!" Kevin exhaled a big sigh of relief.

"Everything okay?" asked Lex, and Kevin nodded. He didn't have enough breath to speak.

Josh dismounted and took off the colorful rope that hung around Cherish's neck.

"Here, tie this to his halter," he said, handing the rope to Kevin. "Then you can lead him beside you without your arm giving out."

"Thanks a lot. Dude, I'm so glad we got him!" He pointed at Diablo's neck, where only a few single thin strands of his mane hung down sadly. "Isn't that a terrible thing to do? That beautiful mane. It's awful!"

Josh nodded. "Yeah, but it could have been worse. At least hair grows back."

"But it'll take years for them to grow as long as they used to be."

"I think, even if Diablo didn't have any hair at all, Ricki would be happy just knowing that he's still alive and otherwise okay." Lex smiled.

"You're probably right."

Together they rode slowly back.

***

When they had almost reached the abandoned farm, Ricki came running toward them.

Laughing and sobbing at once, she threw her arms around Diablo's neck and hugged him.

"Thank goodness," she breathed. "I have you back again. I –" Then she broke down sobbing, and all the fear she had been holding in over the last few hours flowed from her eyes as tears.

"I just want to go home with him," she stammered, and was about to lead him away when Pepe called out, "Hey! Stay here! Your guy Sean, from Mercy Ranch, is on his way with a horse trailer. And the police, by the way." He pointed at Cooper, whom he had tied to a tree with the lasso, as if he had tied him to a stake.

"You have to have a little fun," he chuckled. "He's lucky I'm a cowboy and not an Indian like in those old cheesy movies, otherwise I'd have had his scalp, same as Diablo's!"

"I have to get out of here," whispered Ricki, whose heart was pounding as she looked at Cooper.

"Then let's walk behind the farmhouse and wait for Sean," suggested Kevin. Accompanied by Gwen and Cheryl, they led their horses out of Cooper's view.

"How did you find us?" Ricki finally asked, and Gwen gave her the cell phone they had found near Cooper's car.

"Through your cell phone," she replied. "And thankfully, you lost it here and not at Echo Lake!"

***

For the next two days Ricki was tormented by horrific dreams in which Cooper was chasing her and her horse.

Still, when she woke up covered in sweat, she had the certainty of knowing that her horse was all right and that he was standing calm and comfortable in his stall. It was also good to know that Cooper was going to be institutionalized for a long, long time. He would never again be able to bother her or her horse.

The person who couldn't calm down was old Jake, whose eyes had filled with tears when he saw Diablo without his mane. He couldn't speak. However, when he found out what had happened, he was astonished by Ricki's courage, and as glad as she was that the horse he had known since its birth had not suffered anything worse than the loss of his mane.

The following morning Jake appeared in the stable with a pair of scissors and a razor. He cut off the remaining strands of hair and shaved the rest of it so it was even.

"So, at least now the mane can grow back one length. You'll see, my boy, it'll be okay!" he promised Diablo and patted his muscular neck.

But as glad as Ricki was that her horse had survived Cooper's horrible attack, she was even more fearful, as were her friends, for Carlotta's life. She was to be awakened out of her artificial sleep that day.

***

In the early afternoon, Eleanor Highland and Kevin's mother drove to the hospital with anxious hearts. They had no idea what awaited them and each felt a leaden weight in the pit of her stomach.

Sean and the kids, who had gathered at Mercy Ranch, were even more anxious. They would have to wait until Mrs. Highland called and reported on Carlotta's condition.

Lillian got especially quiet as they waited.

Ricki had been watching her friend with concern for quite a while. Now she stood up and went to sit next to her. Affectionately, she put her arm around her.

"Are you okay?" she asked softly, and Lillian nodded.

"Yeah, I'm okay."

"Hmmm."

"'Hmmm' what?" Lillian sighed. "You know, what I'd like to do is go to the hospital. I wish I could sit by Carlotta's bed and talk with her, like she did when I was in the hospital after the accident. She gave me courage when I didn't know if I would be able to keep my leg or not."

Of course, thought Ricki, *that terrible time had to be passing through her thoughts*.

"Try to name one of us whom she hasn't helped in some way," commented Ricki. "Carlotta knows all of us better than we know ourselves, and it's unbelievable the way she always manages to help us or convince us that there's no problem we can't solve."

Lillian struggled with her emotions.

"That's just it. Carlotta was there for us day and night. She supported us, helped us, comforted us. No matter what was going on, she always made time for us. Oh, Ricki, can you please tell me why it's always the good ones who get hurt, while the rest of us just stand around helpless, knowing there's nothing we can do?"

Ricki considered her question.

"I think everyone is confronted with something terrible, at least once in their lives, that they just have to get through on their own, and no one else can do anything to change it."

Lillian laughed uncomfortably.

"That's something Carlotta would have said." Then, in a rush of emotion, she started to cry. "Ricki, I want to see her.

142

I want to talk with her. I want to tell her that she can't give up because we all need her. We do, and so do the horses, and … just everything. She can't let this beat her. She has to fight. She just has to get better. Do you understand me? She just can't die because of this stupid tumor. That wonderful woman doesn't deserve that. I don't want her to die!" Lillian hugged her friend and cried softly on her shoulder.

Ricki gulped back her own tears. Of course, she'd had similar thoughts over the last several days, but she never managed to speak as openly about them as Lillian had just done.

She was silent. What could she say? It wasn't in her hands or anyone else's to decide whether Carlotta lived or died. If that were possible, then Carlotta would be immortal. All she could do was hold Lillian and comfort her.

However, in spite of her own feelings, Lillian sensed that Ricki had a problem talking about death, and so she blew her nose and tried to change the subject.

"Has Kevin said anything about when Sean and his mother are going to get married?"

"Nope. He hasn't said one word about it." Ricki pretended to be at ease, and was glad that Lillian had given her the opportunity to change the subject. But inside she felt the same as the others. A secret fear was lodged in her heart and she knew that anything she said now would sound silly and phony. Her true thoughts really were with Carlotta, and that was the way it should be.

The kids and Sean were sitting in Carlotta's office staring at the telephone on her desk. While they hoped that Kevin's mother would call them, they were thinking, with

143

much love and hopeful wishes, of the woman who had always put others, human and animal, first in her life.

"Do you remember how furious she was when someone slit her tires?"

"Yeah, and how she got Cathy to overcome her fear of riding Rashid."

"Or how we met Carlotta ... Do you remember when the circus was here in town and she decided to buy Sharazan and Rashid?"

"Wow, that all seems so long ago."

Lillian stood up. "Hey, people, this is starting to sound like a memorial. I think it's awful to speak of Carlotta in the past. I have to get out of here. I feel like the walls are closing in on me!" She ran outside.

Ricki wanted to go after her but Sean held her back.

"Let her be for a while. She'll come back when her thoughts settle down a bit."

"You think so?"

"Yes, I do." Then he stood up. "It won't help if we just sit around here. Carlotta wouldn't like that at all. Especially when there's work to do. So, let's feed the horses. When you're busy, the time goes faster. I don't think anyone will call for at least an hour."

The kids nodded and went outside quietly.

Usually Mercy Ranch was full of laughter; today it was as silent as a tomb, as the young people prepared the stalls for the night.

***

"The intake of medicine has been reduced and now we just have to wait and see if she wakes up on her own," the doctor had said to Caroline and Eleanor. That was over two hours ago, however, and still Carlotta hadn't moved at all.

144

The two women stared through the room's enclosed plate-glass window at their friend.

Mrs. Highland was extremely tense. Caroline, on the other hand, forced herself to keep her emotions in check.

After a long while, Mrs. Highland began to pace back and forth, her face drawn with worry.

"Why doesn't she wake up?" she asked suddenly, nervously wringing her hands. "Something's wrong, isn't it? Anyway, it's driving me crazy, standing here and staring through this glass box at her lying so still. Where's the doctor? I have to speak with the doctor." She signaled the nurse.

"I'm sorry, the doctor can't be disturbed right now."

"What? I've never heard of such a thing. In a hospital, the doctor should be available at all times. Is he performing surgery?"

"No, but –"

"He's not? Then please tell him that I would like to speak to him," Eleanor, having composed herself, said in her most formidable voice.

"I can't leave here," the nurse said defensively, sensing that she was no match for Mrs. Charles Osgood Highland III.

"Then call him. Have him paged. Beep him! ... I don't care what you do, but tell him that I do not intend to just stand here and observe my friend drifting farther and farther away without having someone check on her!"

Caroline approached the nurse and tried to excuse Eleanor's words with a calm glance, and then she turned to the older woman.

"Please, Mrs. Highland, it does no good to make a scene. I'm sure everything humanly possible is being done for Carlotta. And don't forget that she isn't the only patient at this hospital for whom the doctor has to care."

"Yes, yes, I know." Eleanor turned away brusquely. Of course, she knew that Caroline was absolutely right, but the entire situation was making her feel terribly helpless, and she was not a woman who liked being helpless. It made her aggressive.

"She looks so peaceful, don't you think so?" Caroline gently asked, trying to calm Carlotta's oldest friend.

"Too peaceful." Eleanor Highland struggled with herself. "Carlotta once saved my life," she said quietly, more to herself than to her companion. "And now I'm forced to stand here and stare through this glass, and I can't even hold her hand so that she can feel she isn't alone. You can't know how much this is destroying me."

Then she began to tell Caroline about the past, the terrible times when Carlotta and Eleanor held together through thick and thin.

"There was nothing that could have ended our friendship," Mrs. Highland finished after a while and wiped the tears from her eyes. "I don't want her to die without telling her that she was the best friend ... *is* the best friend anyone could wish for!"

There was an emotionally charged silence in the corridor outside Carlotta's room when Eleanor finished her story. Only when the nurse blew her nose loudly did Mrs. Highland swing around. Directly behind the nurse stood the doctor, who cleared his throat awkwardly.

"There you are! I –" Eleanor began, but the doctor went to the utility closet next to Carlotta's room and took out a green hospital gown, a face mask, a hair net, and a pair of latex gloves, and pointed to the shoe protectors that were on the floor.

"Put these on and then go to her," he said, handing over the protective articles. "If Mrs. Mancini really is as you

146

described her, then she'd take my head off if she found out that I refused to let you in her room!"

He tried to smile and, before leaving, he said, "But only five minutes. Not a minute longer! ... And with all my heart, I wish for both of you that your friendship will last many more years." Then his beeper went off and he walked away quickly.

Eleanor and Caroline watched him go in amazement.

"All right, get going." Kevin's mother helped her into the gown. "And when you talk with her, tell her that we all want her to come home to us. Tell her that Sean and I won't get married until she's home again. We want her to be our witness. She ... and you, Eleanor. Tell her that we need her and that we love her. And that the horses at the ranch won't be happy until she's back."

Eleanor stared at Caroline, speechless, and then she gave her a big hug.

"Thank you," she said, touched by Caroline's words. Then, fully covered in hospital green, she went into Carlotta's room and sat down on a chair next to her bed.

Very gently she stroked her friend's fingers and then put her hand over her friend's hand.

She struggled against her tears, trying to find the right words. Finally, pulling herself together, she whispered, "Carlotta, what are you doing? You had a tumor and you didn't tell me. You must have thought, yet again, that you could take care of it yourself, didn't you?" She paused and took a deep breath. "A long, long time ago, we swore that we would be friends forever, and now I get the feeling that you just want to leave without saying good-bye. You know that I can't allow that. You are my best friend in the world ... We aren't so young any more, but we still have lots to look forward to in this life. You have your ranch and I have my stud farm. So fight, Carlotta. Don't just lie here as though your life is over. It's not your time to go. Do you hear me? Caroline and Sean don't want to get married until you can act as their witness. The kids at the ranch are lost without you, and I –" Eleanor smiled painfully, "I couldn't even imagine my life without you. So don't you dare give up, Carlotta. Come back to us!" Eleanor could no longer hold back her tears. And as they fell from her cheeks, one of them landed on Carlotta's hand.

"I don't want to lose you," whispered Mrs. Highland, and she closed her eyes for a moment to regain control.

Suddenly she felt a faint movement in Carlotta's fingers. She held her breath.

"Carlotta? Carlotta!" Come back!" she murmured tensely.

"Your ... Highness ... talks ... too ... much!" Almost inaudibly, and with only a breath of quiet whispering, Carlotta came back to life.

***

Almost a year later wedding bells pealed for Caroline and Sean.

Together with Carlotta and Mrs. Highland, the wedding couple drove to the town hall in a fairytale carriage, followed by all the young riders who came and went daily at Mercy Ranch. They had brushed their horses to a shine and braided their tails and manes with flowers. Behind them came the Western riders and, following them, a few of the bridal couple's friends in decorated cars.

All together they made a lovely picture as they progressed through the town.

When the wedding party arrived at the town hall, Manuela was standing in front with her camera at the ready.

She was going to create a lasting record of this wonderful day on film and in photos, which Caroline and Sean could enjoy for many years to come.

"So, help an old lady out of here," called out Carlotta, and she allowed Sean and Kieran to lift her down from the carriage and into a wheel chair that Manuela had brought for her. "Actually, you're supposed to carry your bride over the threshold, not lift old women around," she winked at Sean.

Always ready with a response, he kissed her cheek and said, "You can't have too much practice before carrying someone over the threshold."

Laughing, the wedding party entered the town hall with their witnesses and friends, while the riders outside formed an avenue of horses.

"Do you remember, just a year ago ..." Ricki tugged at Diablo's short mane, beaming at Lillian.

"Yes. Exactly one year ago it was Carlotta's second birthday!" Lillian's big smile told everyone how happy she was. "Oh, it's so wonderful that she survived!"

"Did she ever," joked Cheryl. "You wouldn't have believed how she sailed through the stable this morning in her wheel chair, checking out every horse and stall, and then scolded us because there was a piece of hay caught in Sheila's tail. Oh, it is good to have her back."

"She's really accepted that thing pretty well, don't you think?" Cathy commented.

"The wheel chair? Oh, no. Definitely no!" Ricki laughed. "She set herself a goal that she'll be limping around on her crutch by next year at the latest. She said she had had a tumor in her head and she didn't need another one in her backside from all this sitting."

The kids burst out laughing.

"Look out, they're coming," Kieran called, and as though on command, the seated riders raised arches of colorful roses between the rows of horses, for the bridal couple to walk through.

"Long live the bride and the groom!" called out Kevin, overjoyed. He gave his mother a kiss in front of everyone and poked his stepfather in the ribs playfully.

"Long live Sean and Caroline," said Carlotta more quietly, "the new owners of Mercy Ranch. I wish you a long, happy, and healthy life together!" Then with a joyful gleam in her eyes she removed an envelope from her purse and handed over the transfer-of-ownership papers to the bridal couple.

"So! From now on I intend to spend my time relaxing and let the two of you work." She laughed. "But don't think I'm not going to go into the stable. I guarantee that someday I am going to ride again, even if you have to tie me to the saddle!"

"That's the Carlotta we know."

"Long live Carlotta!" shouted Kevin again, and everyone joined in.

"Silly boy," replied the former ranch owner, moved by the outpouring of love. "But before he says anything else stupid, and I steal the show from the bride and groom, let's ride back home. I'm really looking forward to a huge piece of that wonderful wedding cake."

And with the laughter and joy of that wonderful day, the
story of Ricki and her marvelous black horse, Diablo,
has come to an end. But that wouldn't quite be right. I'm
convinced that Diablo has become immortal in your hearts.
Whenever you feel like it, let him gallop on in your thoughts
– always toward the sun and toward your own personal
happiness.

My heartfelt wishes to all of you!

Yours,
Gabi Adam